UNETHICAL CONDUCT

A Terry McGuire Thriller

ARTHUR COLE &
NIGEL C. WILLIAMS

WORDCATCHER publishing

D1323669

Unethical Conduct
A Terry McGuire Thriller – Book 1

© 2018 Arthur Cole & Nigel C. Williams
Source images supplied by Adobe Stock
Cover design © 2018 David Norrington

British Library Cataloguing in Publication Data.
A catalogue record for this book is available from the British Library.

Published in the United Kingdom by Wordcatcher Publishing Group Ltd
www.wordcatcher.com
Tel: 02921 888321
Facebook.com/WordcatcherPublishing

First Edition: 2018, published by Artcymru Publications
Second Edition: 2019, Wordcatcher Publishing, revised and re-edited

Print edition ISBN: 9781789420654
Ebook edition ISBN: 9781789420661

Category: Crime Thriller

"The accomplice to the crime of corruption
is frequently our own indifference."

Bess Myerson

Terry McGuire Thriller Series

Unethical Conduct

Edge of Integrity

Death and Depravity

Angel of Death

Nest of Vipers

Night Hawker

Redemption

Betrayal

Coming Soon

Raven Conner Investigates

ABOUT THE AUTHORS

Arthur Cole joined the Glamorgan Police at the age of seventeen. At nineteen, he joined the South Wales Constabulary as a constable and was stationed in Bridgend.

After nearly four years working beats, he became a detective constable, covering the whole division.

During his service, he dealt with every kind of major crime committed in the area, including murder and rape, before joining Special Branch where he worked until he retired after thirty years of service, having achieved the rank of detective sergeant. In 1975, he met Caroline, his wife, who was also a serving police officer at the time. Caroline left the Force in 1980 to raise their family. They have two children.

Upon retirement, Arthur became a gardener and enjoys golf and all sports as well as writing poetry. *Unethical Conduct* is his first novel, written in collaboration with Nigel C. Williams.

Nigel joined the Metropolitan Police in 1981 and was posted to Brixton. In 1984, he transferred home to South Wales where he worked beats and became a traffic officer. He was also authorised for the use of firearms and became a VIP and Special Escort Group driver.

In 1994, Nigel was hit by a stolen car on duty, which fractured his spine. During recovery he retrained and achieved a first-class (honours) degree in fine art. He then gained a teaching qualification from Cardiff University and a master's degree from Swansea, where he now lectures.

Nigel has been married to Caroline for twenty-seven years and has three children, a granddaughter, and a dog called Zac.

This is Nigel's second collaboration, the first being *No Step Back* with Alan Lloyd MBE.

FOREWORD

Real-life policing isn't like TV and films. There isn't always the luxury of ten-man teams working on just one case. In fact, officers manage caseloads of crimes and these compete for their time. These thrillers are drama, but they are based on real-world policing in South Wales, spanning several decades. Names and situations may have been fictionalised, but the crimes and criminals are lifelike enough. If the plots seem fantastic, remember the adage that fact is stranger than fiction.

PROLOGUE

The lights of a Ford Transit van cut through the dark, cold winter air, windscreen wipers valiantly battling against the heavy, near-horizontal rain. Its diesel engine grumbled, and the chassis creaked and moaned as it trundled and bounced along the pockmarked lane. It pulled to a stop at a secluded corner of an empty car park overlooking the beach and the thunderous sea beyond. Only the occasional angry breaking wave could be heard in the inky night.

It wasn't unusual to see the shapes of cars parked there in the early hours of the morning, many rhythmically rocking and bouncing to a beat generated by their amorous occupants. But not tonight. The winter weather had deterred lovers, stargazers and devotees of nocturnal seaside walks. Tonight, the car park was the exclusive domain of the old Ford van.

The rattling engine fell silent. The occupants listened for several minutes to the sound of the breaking waves far out in the shallow bay.

Three silhouettes jumped from the cab and hurriedly opened the rear doors. Two of the shadowy figures pulled a heavy, plastic wrapped package from the cargo hold and lugged it towards the beach, dropping it awkwardly off the black-top hard-standing onto the wet sand three feet below. The third figure held a shovel and remained near the van, keeping watch.

Satisfied the coast was clear, the third shadow also dropped down onto the beach and followed the heavy package as it was dragged along the gravel and silt to an outcrop of low, black rocks anchored deep within the fine sand several yards further out towards the incoming sea.

The third shadow dug a large hole; seven feet long by three feet wide and two feet deep. It took nearly fifteen minutes before the hole was deep enough to take the heavy, plastic-wrapped package.

* * *

"As a copper, you know, it's not unusual to have a complaint made against you. I've heard so many say that a copper isn't doing his or her job unless they've got a string of complaints on their personnel records." Alan Chambers sipped from his pint of lager and set the glass down carefully on a paper drip mat before continuing, his soft voice barely registering his Liverpool roots. "The service has changed so much since I joined. Villains used to fear *and* respect the police – not any more. Everyone knows their rights now and everyone knows how to complain, even if their grievance dates back to the time of Adam and Eve. Compensation is the new get-rich-quick scheme. It's better than ISAs or the sodding lottery."

He shook his head sadly and gazed at the shiny trophies proudly displayed on the shelf above the large picture window overlooking the eighteenth green. "It's now part of everyday life. Screw anyone and everyone for anything you can get."

The man sitting quietly opposite him shrugged and drained the last of his pint of Guinness.

"We all know that some complaints against the police are frivolous nonsense," Assistant Chief Constable Chambers continued, "but every now and again something comes along to make me sit up and take notice, something that threatens to undermine my belief in this job." Chambers noticed the empty glass of his companion and drained his own. "Your round, I think?"

The other man stood, brushed the remains of a stale pasty from his pale blue golf trousers and straightened his jumper before strolling to the bar for a refill.

Chambers sat quietly, watching the other club members laughing and generally enjoying Captain's Day at the Porthcawl Golf Club. He had taken up golf late in life but had still managed to drop his handicap to single figures. His partner for the day had pushed him close over the eighteen holes – but not close enough.

The drinks returned and Chambers' playing partner sat once more.

"You'd think coppers would make good criminals, wouldn't you?" Chambers said. "Lost count of the times I've heard the old chestnut, 'it takes a thief to catch a thief,' and all that bollocks. Well, there have been too many coppers who have gone to the dark side during their careers but it's surprising how pretty inept most of them were. The main failings seem to be brought about by arrogance. They don't cover their tracks like they've seen the villains try to do so many times. It's all down to a belief that they're somehow above the law. They aren't and never will be. I for one will not sit back and watch the good name of so many decent men and women get dragged through the dirt for bent bastards masquerading as officers of the law."

His partner finally spoke. "And what has this got to do with me?"

* * *

The three men patted down the sand over the package they had buried and ran back to the Transit van.

The driver was perhaps ten years older than the other two, who were sat, wet and shivering, alongside each other on the front seats.

The old diesel engine misfired, then coughed and spluttered into life. The van rocked as the driver crunched the gears into reverse and quickly turned it around. The tyres spun as the van took off from the car park and sped back down the secluded lane.

As the red tail-lights faded into the distance, the first of the incoming waves began to lick at the mound of sand created by the recent nocturnal visitors. A small tumble of sand rode away with the retreating wave before another swept in and stole more grains. After a dozen or so increasingly powerful rollers, a section of plastic was revealed. After another dozen waves had snatched away the sand, what was clearly a human hand protruded from a split in the plastic shroud.

* * *

Chambers took a long swallow of his fresh pint of lager and stared at his companion. "No flies on you," he smiled.

"I know you didn't invite me here today for my golfing prowess."

Chambers' smile faded quickly. "True."

"Then tell me, what the hell is going on?"

The ACC sat forward, his face close to the man opposite and he looked quickly around him. Satisfied nobody was listening, he beckoned the man to lean in even closer. "I want you to do a job for me."

"And you've brought me here, to a golf club, to ask me? Why not call me into the office?"

"Don't want to do that just yet. Don't want to make it official, until I know you're interested."

"I'm interested."

"Okay. I'll get the files together. Nobody must know about this, understand?"

"Shit!" The man slumped back in his chair and his shoulders sagged. "Shit!" he cursed again. "Internal investigation?"

Chambers nodded. "I need someone I can trust, a DI with no black marks. I know you're playing off the same tee as me. I know I can trust you, Terry."

"What do you want me to do?"

Smiling, Chambers gulped down his pint and held out his hand. "Finish that off, I'll get you another. Now I know you're on-side we'll meet in my office tomorrow and I'll give you the full SP."

1

The holiday season was over for the Trecco Bay Caravan Park, but many of the owners still used their retreats throughout most of the year. They had to vacate for six weeks, to comply with the law but, on the whole, there was always life in Porthcawl, even if sometimes that life could be pretty low on the evolutionary scale.

Gwladys and Fred Thomas walked along the edge of the huge, sunken, grass bowl the locals called 'The Arena'. At one time it accommodated touring caravans and was completely surrounded by large mobile homes that were ironically called 'statics'. The Arena was a little larger than a running track and the base was flat and circular and about fifteen to twenty feet below the rest of the old Sandy Bay Park. Sandy Bay had closed down many years ago. Only its close neighbour, Trecco Bay, now remained active and it continued to attract holidaymakers to Porthcawl each year.

Fred Thomas bought his first caravan in 1973, at a time when Trecco and Sandy Bay were at their peak. The fairground attraction nearby was great for the kids and, as a collier from the Rhondda Valley, it was handy to pop over to the van as often as his shifts would allow. Many of the miners in the South Wales coalfield had invested money in caravans at the parks. It was good to take in fresh sea air after breathing coal dust for most of their working days.

It was sad to see what had happened to Sandy Bay and it was sad to see the fairground in a state of decline. It hadn't been the same since the big theme parks began popping up around the country; and a terrible accident on one of the attractions had claimed the life of a child about twenty years before.

Package holidays to Spain and destinations further afield had also chipped away at Porthcawl's attraction and the inconsistent summer weather of South Wales seemed to add misery to an already difficult situation.

However, Trecco had experienced a recent revival in fortunes. Investment in the caravan park and club facilities had helped to improve things considerably.

Gwladys Thomas loved her daily constitutional. Since Fred had retired shortly after Thatcher's decimation of the coal industry, they had spent most of their time in the various caravans they had bought since. Their new caravan was like nothing they could ever have imagined back in the early seventies. Now they had double glazing, central heating, bathrooms that were plumbed to the mains water and sewerage, a kitchen better than most homes, and decked areas to sit and watch the sea – when the weather was nice enough. By comparison, the first van they'd bought had three previous owners, gas mantle lights that often burned away in inexperienced hands, and a coal fire that would cause a coronary for most Health and Safety professionals today.

Even though they had been married for over forty

years, they still walked hand in hand. Fred had always been a bit of a romantic and loved to make Gwladys feel special. He hadn't been feeling too good of late. Many of his former workmates had died early or succumbed to a debilitating lung disease of one kind or another. The pneumoconiosis played hell with his chest and he had slowed down. But Gwladys was still fit and was true to their wedding vows, looking after him no matter what life threw at them.

They walked away from the edge of The Arena and began to follow the road towards the sea and back to their caravan on the front, when Gwladys saw something moving fast in her peripheral vision. She stopped and Fred did the same.

"What is it, bach?" he puffed.

"Did you see that?"

"See what?"

Then Fred saw.

Running at full speed between the vans was a naked man. He disappeared behind one of the mobile homes and then appeared again on the other side, about a hundred yards away from them.

"My God," Gwladys said, "he's naked."

"I can bloody see that," Fred fumed.

The naked man stood facing them and began to play with a body part that unexpectedly did not feel the chill of a November in Porthcawl.

Fred and Gwladys were momentarily dumbstruck. Neither had experienced anything like it in their lives.

"You... dirty... bastard!" Fred spluttered and coughed. Had he been ten years younger he'd have chased the pervert and given him a good hiding, but all he could do was turn Gwladys away from the sight and wait for the flasher to disappear.

2

I knew only too well that I was up to my neck in some really serious shit.

The ACC 'Crime' had dropped a real humdinger on me. Talk about stress, I didn't know whether I was coming or going.

Anyway, I had got the call direct from the Assistant Chief Constable. I was expecting it – after what he had told me at the golf club – but his tone on the phone was certainly not as relaxed as it had been over a few pints.

"Terry? Get your arse up here a bit sharpish, the shit has hit the fan... big time... and I need a bloke with a pair of balls, who can keep his trap shut," he said.

Okay, I confess, he didn't quite say all that, but that was the essence of the conversation. The ACC, Alan Chambers, was an 'up-and-comer,' only been in our Force about twelve months. Came from Merseyside, he was a real Scouser – but without the accent. He was an average-looking bloke, no real distinguishing features. Still had all his dark brown hair and kept himself fit with a regular game of golf and an early morning swim. Born and bred in Toxteth, you could say he had slipped through the net and taken the straight and narrow path. First time I met him was in a CID conference, I had instantly liked him: he talked my language, a real copper's copper.

Anyway, I popped up to the 'Big House' and waited

to be given the nod before I entered his teak-clad office.

"Sit down, Terry," he said amiably, when I finally got the call to enter.

I did as I was told and waited. I knew I had been summoned to speak to him about some internal investigation but had no idea about the specifics.

The Assistant Chief Constable was flicking through his iPhone. I grinned as I got this odd image in my mind of him watching porn on his device. I often got daft thoughts like that from time to time, bit silly, but it broke the monotony of waiting for senior officers – something I had been doing a lot of recently.

"Did you have any dealings with a now-retired DI by the name of Chris Coulter?" he finally asked. "Seems he spent most of his time on Division and the last four or five on the Drug Squad. He retired a few months ago."

"Do I know him? Too royal, sir, never worked with him but I know he was a sharp bastard. Played his cards close to his chest and I always had my doubts about him."

"Well, it looks like you weren't far off the mark. Had a complaint about him, alleging all sorts of corruption, protection rackets, and one count of rape."

It didn't surprise me. "Sounds about right," I said. Then I realised it wasn't what the ACC wanted to hear. "Sorry, boss!"

The ACC shook his head and held his hands in the air, inviting me to continue.

"Who's the complainant?"

"Not just one complainant, Terry, but two. Both career criminals and both put away by Coulter years ago for drugs and burglary. Say they were fitted up."

"That old chestnut," I scoffed. "Any names, boss?"

The ACC checked his phone again; *so it wasn't porn he was looking at.*

"Victor Edward Thomas and Peter Geoffrey Samuels... with a G not a J."

"I've done the pair of them, years ago. Raves from the graves," I nodded.

"I know, Terry. You're the only one they'll talk to. They said... and I quote... 'Terry's a bit of a twat, but he's straight as a die and he'll sort it for us.'"

"I don't know what to say to that."

The ACC laughed and dropped his phone onto the desk.

"Boss, they're small potatoes. Having said that, they've got all the contacts, and done a fair bit of bird. Have they given times, dates or anything?"

"No, Terry. That'll be down to you. I've got nothing else. I don't need to tell you that this is very delicate. It's even more so now because Coulter is getting a lot of press due to the fact that he's become a local councillor and he's flying the old 'crime reduction' flag," he punctuated the air with his index fingers. "Bit ironic, but if things pan out he can fucking fly it in the nick with the old lags he's fitted up."

"Have I got a free hand, boss? You know the way I work. How many men can you give me?"

"Only one, Terry, and that's it. You report direct to me. I've spoken to Ron, he says he won't interfere. Update me... say... every two weeks? No phone calls, we meet in person."

I took the hint. Meeting over. I shook his hand and detected a Masonic influence in there. Once outside, I stopped and looked up at the ceiling and imagined some wonderful golden place in the sky with golden ghosts sticking two fingers up at me and laughing. I leaned against the wall and sighed.

You're killing me, and my marriage.

3

I spent a few hours trawling through the personnel files with my pal, Dai. I should say that I got Dai to trawl through the files and read them to me. Privilege of rank... I'm not bloody stupid.

My right-hand man, DS Dai Williams, a career detective and brilliant investigator, offered to help me out and I would have liked to keep him on the case, but I knew I couldn't argue the addition of a detective sergeant for the enquiry, at least not yet. To be honest, I hoped the complaint would turn out to be a load of bullshit. Villains were always complaining about coppers, over all sorts of trivial bollocks and, at that moment, even though Coulter was a twat, I had no reason to think otherwise in this case.

I liked Dai. He never took any prisoners and didn't give a monkey's about anyone, criminal or senior officer alike. When I say 'he didn't take any prisoners' I'm referring to his attitude rather than his arrests. Far from it, Dai was actually a prolific thief-taker, one of the best. His only weakness was the ladies; married twice, divorced twice, *say no more*. His problem was that he was too good looking, not that I'd ever tell him that, of course. But it was true. Wherever he went he seemed to have some woman in close proximity. He was the original babe magnet and he seemed to be eternally on the pull. His hair was always what I would call 'designer scruffy' and he had a face that would make Tom Cruise envious. He had it all on the looks front and had a sharp mind with a wicked sense of humour. However, I guessed it was his air of self-confidence that was irresistible to the ladies.

Dai began to read his notes. "Coulter joined the job in 1982 as a cadet. He was from a wealthy family; his parents had their own furniture removal business, so he never wanted for anything."

Unlike me, I thought. I had to fight for everything as I grew up. Perhaps that's why I never suffered fools.

"He joined the regular force in December 1984 and, after his initial training, got a posting to Cardiff Central. During his probationary period, he made a bit of a name for himself as a good thief-taker. Commended on ten occasions in the first two years."

I was impressed. That was pretty good by anybody's standards. I don't think I had one commendation in my first three years.

"After his probation, he was attached to the plain-clothes squad down the docks, mainly dealing with druggies and the 'brasses'. Again, it looks like he fitted in well to this type of work and it seems he was destined for a career in crime."

"In more ways than one, if these allegations are to be believed," I added. I stood and walked out of my office with two mugs the size of small buckets ready for a refill from a coffee machine I had bought for the office. Dai and I were alone. The rest of the team had been sent out on various jobs to give us some space.

I returned a few minutes later and set the mugs down in a tiny, clear oasis on my otherwise cluttered desk.

"Two years later," Dai continued, "he requested a transfer back to his home town of Bridgend. This was granted and, in fact, coincided with him being promoted to sergeant. He took up his new position, but after a few months, he was made a detective sergeant on the Drug Squad East, covering nearly half the Force. He was there for about five years and had some cracking results and earned a reputation Force-wide. He was qualified to inspector, then for some reason went back on Division as a DS."

That raised my eyebrows.

Dai spotted my expression. "I found that a bit strange, too, because up until then he was on an upward curve regarding promotion. In fact, it seems he trawled the Division for the next ten years, still reeling in the commendations, but no promotion. It was as if he was serving a penance."

"Remind me to dig deeper into that blip," I said. "Must be a reason."

Dai nodded and continued, "In 2003, he was eventually promoted to inspector and spent the next couple of years in the operations room."

"I bet that pissed him off," I sniped. "No commendations forthcoming in there."

"I think he used to write his own," Dai chuckled.

I made a claw-shape with my hand and the sound of a cat. "Oh, we're catty, jealous bastards."

"From there he was made the DI in Bridgend," Dai said, "a post he held for the next six years. Then on to the Drug Squad where he finished his service."

"All in all, not a bad career," I observed. Knowing what I did, I could attest to the fact that Coulter was one smooth operator and if what was alleged was true, he was going to be very difficult to bring to book. Flies certainly stayed away from him.

* * *

Freddie Mercury belted out the chorus for 'Fat Bottomed Girls' as Cynthia Matthews cleared the dishes from the dining table. Even though it had rained for most of the day, she had enjoyed the short break.

Her father sat in an armchair in a corner of the caravan watching the television with earphones pressed into place to hear the latest news. Her mother had retired to a bedroom for forty winks whilst Cynthia and her younger sister, Mandy, cleared up.

The meal had been good. Steak and kidney pie had always been her parents' favourite, not that Cynthia was too keen on it. Still, she didn't get to see her parents often and she had been happy to go along with the menu for the evening.

Cynthia and Mandy danced to the music blasting from the iPod speaker as they fed the dishes into the compact dishwasher. The caravan was less than a year old and had every conceivable mod con. Her dad had bought the van for her parents' golden wedding anniversary and it was a vast improvement on the last one they had. Cynthia had never really liked caravan holidays and had never been too keen on Trecco Bay, but the place had changed beyond recognition in recent years. She was beginning to see the appeal; after all, her parents loved the place and that was all that really mattered, and even the weather hadn't spoiled their week.

She was sad to be leaving for Dubai the next day, back to her salon and her wealthy clients, but tonight would be good, she was going to ensure that. Life in Dubai had been good to her and she loved it whilst she was there but it was always hard to say goodbye to family, especially when her parents were not getting any younger. She missed her mother, father and sister but she had built a new life in a new country, a life that was far removed from the one she had lived in Wales. Yes, it was great to come home but, if she were honest with herself, she was happier in Dubai.

A knock at the window behind her startled her. Cynthia walked to the door and opened it to find a man walking away, a man who was not wearing any clothes. He stopped twenty yards away and turned to expose himself to her.

4

I had to get me a good wingman for the Coulter case, preferably a DC with a bit about him who could come and go as he liked without being missed; a bit of a ghost. I'd have preferred to have had my DS working with me but as the ACC wanted the enquiry below the radar I knew I'd have to go for a DC with no obvious connections to me or Coulter. At least I knew that Dai would look after the office in my absence.

As it happened, I knew just the bloke to help me.

I popped in to see the ACC. It would have been much easier to ring him, but he told me not to. Who was I to argue?

"I want John Fuller on this job with me, boss. He's Special Branch and he's my man. He's got the lot in his drawer – surveillance trained, cracking investigator, and not afraid to push the boundaries."

"I'll sort it and he'll be with you tomorrow," was Chambers' reply. That was encouraging.

I needed a good drink, so I rang the missus, gave her the usual load of old bollocks about needing to unwind and then popped straight to the boozer. I enjoyed the occasional 'social' gathering with colleagues after a hard day at work but I was aware that it could become a habit. I had recently heard of a woman inspector who had hit the bottle a little too hard and had stripped off on a table in a local boozer after a particularly heavy session. She had even verbally abused a senior officer who had graced the function with his presence. I never liked the superintendent myself but I did like Julia, the DI. Julia was now working at a desk somewhere and that was a shame. She was a damn good detective.

I got home about midnight, slinked into bed and cwtshed up to a cold arse. Story of my life.

* * *

The following morning, I got to the office and John Fuller was waiting for me.

"Morning, boss. Must be a real pearler for you to ask for me," he grinned.

I nodded. "That's an understatement, butt."

I shut my office door behind us and entered my quiet mode. I warned him that what I was about to say had to remain between us.

John was also well put together, handsome, been on the Branch for years, a real handful, and I often wondered if he had some of Dai's DNA because the women loved him, too. He sat opposite me in the chair Dai had occupied the previous day.

"This is the score, John," I said quietly. "Two chancers by the name of Victor Edward Thomas and Peter Geoffrey Samuels... that's Geoff with a 'G' and not with a 'J'..." - I grinned as I recalled the ACC's unnecessary elaboration – "have come out of the woodwork and are alleging that a retired DI, Chris

Coulter, fitted them both up and has been involved in supplying drugs. There's even mention of a rape."

"Bloody hell, boss. Chris Coulter? I've heard of him. Never had anything to do with him, but he had a bit of a reputation, and not all good."

"Right. Let's get some background. Dai Williams and I have done the checks on Coulter. I want you to get me full antecedents on the pair making the allegations; their arrests, their times in the nick, who did them? Everything. Times and dates will be important on this one, John, it's got to be airtight, butt. Take a couple of days and then come back to me."

I watched John leave the office and stared at the picture sitting on my table. The silver frame was in need of a good clean and several layers of dust partially obscured the image of my wife and me sitting on the wall of some fishing port somewhere in Devon with our two children. The kids were only six or seven at the time and both looked as miserable in the image as I was feeling as I thought about what we might unearth about Coulter. No copper wanted to have to arrest a colleague, but I had always believed that oily scum always rose to the surface, eventually, and when that happened, someone had to take responsibility for scooping it up and getting rid of it. It seemed that I had won the not-so-coveted scum-ladle.

I called home and spoke to Molly, my wife. I told her I'd be home for dinner – for a change. I had no intention of working long hours on this job, unless there was no other option. Molly had lived with me for so long that she no longer seemed to have a problem with me working the irregular hours.

I checked the addresses on file for the two complainants. I would have to speak to them at some point and the sooner I did that the better.

Later that morning, I made my way to Blaencaerau, a council estate about ten miles from Bridgend. Formerly built as a village of terraced houses to serve the coal miners and their families, like so many other villages in South Wales, Blaencareau became a focus for the council housing explosion of the fifties and sixties. More houses followed over the decades and, what were once new and exciting properties for the community, gradually began falling into disrepair through lack of badly needed investment. Many of my colleagues believed the place to be rough. I suppose, to an outsider, it was, but my family were from a village like Blaencaerau and I always felt at home in places like that. I understood them. I spoke their language.

I was on my way to see Victor Edward Thomas in my pool-car. He wasn't expecting me, so I didn't know how he'd react.

I parked the car and immediately, like an army of sloths, the locals appeared from under their rocks.

"Any of you fuckers touch that car and I promise you, I'll chop your fucking hands off," I shouted.

I heard a distant voice amongst the gathering group of yobs that would have looked at home in that Star Wars bar, "Listen to him? He's fucking off it."

I looked around and I spotted Vic pushing through

the assembled aliens.

"How you doing, Terry? Long time no see. Fancy a cuppa?"

"Not unless you've recently done a City and Guilds course in hygiene."

Vic shook my hand and my comment about his hygiene seemed to fly way over the head of the scruffy, dirty bastard. I followed him into the house.

The smell that greeted me almost made me puke. Stale, sweaty clothes mixed with a soupçon of damp and a liberal sprinkling of cat piss never really appealed to me. I was glad I turned down the cup of tea.

"You come about that bent bastard, Coulter, I hope?"

"Sure have, Vic. Is it on the up or a load of old pony?"

Victor pretended to be offended at the question. "Oh, it's on the up, Terry. Make no fucking bones about that."

Was he telling me the truth or was there some other underlying agenda at work? He was a villain, after all, and villains and coppers were, *usually*, on different teams. "Look, Vic, I want you and Samuels to come down to the nick, so we can sort it all out."

"'Sort it all out', Terry? He's a fucking menace, he's put innocent blokes away and it's about time he paid the fucking price."

"Reel that in a minute," I said. "You were never innocent."

"I was for this lot, the stuff he stitched us up for."

I shrugged. "You know he's retired? He's not a copper anymore. He can't do you any more harm."

"Oh aye, he's a lardy-dardy councillor or some bollocks now, saw him on TV last night. That's what riled me and made me want to contact you. But it makes no difference what he is now, he's got it coming. Why should he get to be living it up with other councillors? It's time all those bastards knew who they're swigging Möet with. Me and Sams will call down early tomorrow morning, seven-thirty. Does that suit?"

"No problem with that," I grumbled, "You sure you can get out of bed by that time?"

"Always an early bird, me," he said. "Got to be early, I've got some business meetings all day."

I nearly laughed in his face. "Business?"

He nodded and puffed out his chest. "I like to think of myself as one of those entry-pren-newers," he said. I didn't think he had even heard the word 'entrepreneur' before let alone pronounce it, even if he did get it wrong.

Then I warned him, "But it's all going on tape."

"Why not go the full fucking hog and video it while you're at it?" he snapped. "But there's one condition. We only talk to you, nobody else. This is a can of worms, butt."

"Fair enough," I said, "seven thirty it is." We shook hands and I left quickly so that I could wipe my hand on my trousers.

At least my car was still intact.

5

My head throbbed rhythmically from the effects of a bottle of red wine with my wife the night before as I waited outside the nick for the complainants to arrive and, like two bad pennies but true to their word, Vic and Sams turned up dead on time in a smart-looking, bright-red BMW.

They both looked sheepish when they spotted me outside the main entrance to the station. They left the car parked at a jaunty angle in the street, a prime target for the eager traffic wardens, but who was I to spoil the fun of our ticket-happy brethren? They'd probably be okay though. Our traffic wardens didn't start work until nine and I hoped to have them both done and dusted long before then. Vic locked the car, and both men strolled across the road towards me. Vic shrugged and nodded back towards the car. "Would you believe it's my gran's?"

"No, I fucking wouldn't," I snarled.

I took them up to my office where John was sitting at a desk, messing about on the computer. Victor wasn't happy when he saw my DC.

"Who the fuck is he, Terry? I told you, we won't speak to anyone else. You're all the bloody same," he raged.

I got a bit pissed. Whenever I get annoyed, my volume control gets screwed up and my voice rises to threat-level ten. "Hey, listen to me now, Dick and Dom, you want Coulter? Well, shape up or fuck off out of my sight. You got the message?"

To my surprise, and disappointment, they didn't storm out. They both sat down and I slammed the door shut. I had never had time for any kind of corruption but I really didn't want to be involved in this inquiry. Good, efficient policework depended upon the trust between colleagues. I was sure that some colleagues would think of me differently after something like this. I knew I shouldn't be bothered by that. If I truly believed that corrupt officers had no place in the job, then there was nothing to worry about. But worry I did. It still made me uneasy. What if this was all bollocks? How would a full investigation into serious allegations like this affect Coulter's new career? A great deal was riding on the word of two scrotes.

I took a deep breath and thought about a referee blowing his whistle to kick-start a game. This was my kick-off and there would be no going back until the game was won by one side or the other. Like partisan commentators at an international rugby match, I knew I had to remain impartial, even if I was silently rooting for one side. "Me and John are going to sort this, one way or the other. Two options – either it's a load of shite – or it's true? So, convince me," I said.

Vic looked satisfied. He could clearly read my mood. "If you say your mate's okay, then that's good enough for me."

I nodded and calmed down. I managed to get my volume back to quiet mode again – that's never below threat-level five. I have a voice like Bryn Terfel when I talk but unfortunately not when I sing. "Now this is what's going to happen. We'll interview you individually on tape and after that you can piss off home in that smart Beemer of your gran's and leave it to me. You happy with that?"

They both nodded their heads in time like an intellectually challenged, synchronised swimming team.

"John? Take Samuels next door and bleed him dry... I want everything, every last bit of info."

"Victor? You are mine, butt, and the same thing goes for you." I paused for a moment to catch my breath. "Fuck me, you pair are hard work."

Samuels piped up, "We'd only take that off you, Ter, respect."

"Oh, get out, you bull-shitter," I grinned.

6

I started my interview with Victor at thirty-five minutes past seven. I made a note of the time for reference. I hadn't even opened my mouth before he was off and running – like Sepp Blatter fleeing an expenses enquiry.

"The first time Coulter fitted us up was in 1990, we had a five stretch... the bastard! Someone's got to do something about him. He's evil, a right crooked--"

I held up my hand. "Hang on, Vic. I'll ask the questions. Bloody hell, you know the score."

"Sorry, he's a bad bastard, you know? There are other blokes he's done over and they'll talk as well."

"Okay. But let's do things my way. "Tell me about the first time, Vic."

He didn't seem to be really bothered by my negative attitude towards him. It was clear to me that he was determined to tell his side of a story that I wasn't looking forward to hearing, but I was slowly adjusting to the fact that I had to give him his day.

"Like I said," he continued, "it was 1990, late in the year. Me and Sams were approached to do a job in Porthcawl..."

"What sort of job?"

"A robbery," he looked a little unsure but quickly realised he needed to drag it all out if I was going to believe him. "Well, me and Sams had never been involved in that shit. Of course, we were burglars and car thieves, but nothing heavy. We told the bloke, 'No.

Fuck that shit, that's serious bird.' Anyway, off he toddles. Sams and I thought, 'He's fucking lost the plot.' We'd known him for years, he only had a bit of form, but he'd done a load of jobs, mostly houses." Vic took a swig from the bottle of water I'd brought for him.

"Anyway, a couple of weeks later, me and Sams rent a caravan on Trecco Bay for a couple of weeks. Our intention was to do a few breaks, shops and stuff like that and have a base nearby. We had just done the offie on the estate, down by the lake?" He looked at me as if I knew what off-licence he was referring to. Truth was I didn't have a clue; they seemed to open and close faster than a prozzy's legs.

"Anyway," he continued, "we were back in the van counting the spoils - cash, booze, some ciggies and other bits and bobs. Then there's a knock on the door and we shit ourselves. The next thing we know, in he walks, bold as bollocks. I said, 'Fuck! You scared us shitless, I hope you haven't robbed no fucker?' He's carrying a holdall and puts it on the table."

I was confused. "Who are you talking about, Vic?"

"He's a lifer, Ter, he won't see the light of day, topped an old man in Carmarthen - armed robbery - went tits-up. His name's Steve Diamond. Rumour is that he also killed someone when he was a kid but he was never caught. Anyway, he opens the holdall and says, 'What d'you think, boys?' And there they are... two fucking handguns winking up at us. 'Have a decco boys', he says, and like two fucking lemons we each pick one up. 'Careful, boys, they're loaded', he laughs like some bloody mental bloke. Fuck me, we dropped them back like hot potatoes. 'You better fuck off with them, butt', I told him. He left, laughing his head off.

"I'm sure he must have been on something. The next time we see him is a few days later up at the arcades. He comes on to us about another job. 'Fuck off,' we told him, 'we're not interested.' He said, 'No? It's the bookies on the Esplanade, the till is full on a Friday night, the silly fuckers don't bank it. Jump in the car, we'll take a spin up there.'

"Ten minutes later, we're there." He looked defensive, knowing he'd just admitted to being a daft twat.

"We suss it out and we're in two minds. 'If we do it, what time, Steve?' I ask him. 'About nine-ish, I reckon,' he said. 'Give 'em time to leave the car park and then we're in. They leave a window unlocked around the back, no alarm or fuck all... dull they are. Are you in, boys?' I looked at Sams and said, 'Aye, but no guns.' 'No need for guns,' he said, 'it'll be empty.'

"Anyway, the following night, it's on. We wait for them all to go and Steve does the business. He lets us in the front door and then we're just about to force the till when there's fucking sirens and blue lights everywhere. We scatter and run like hell in all directions.

"We're fucked. They nick Sams and me over by the hotel. Steve got away, but I didn't think anything of it at the time.

"Straight down the nick, straight into the cells. We both thought, 'there's a twelve month up our shirt.'

"But, oh no. Who fucking turns up to interview us? Yeah, you guessed it: it's that arse-bandit, Coulter, and his blond oppo Morse... a king-size, curly-haired twat.'

"He hooks us both into an interview room and on the table are the two hand guns. I looked at Sams and took a sharp intake of breath. It's gone from twelve months to five fucking years in the blink of an eye. Didn't take a lot of working out, did it? That twat, Diamond, had set us up for Coulter. Me and Sams never answered a question on interview. We knew our prints were all over the guns and no fucker would believe us. We had to take it on the chin... more fool us."

"Bloody hell, Vic. I think it's time for a cup of tea," I said. "How much more is there?"

"Only one other bit for me and Sams, a few years later, but it's the other info you'll be interested in."

* * *

A stroll and occasional jog along the beach in the early morning was better than any therapy. Bryn Bowen had experienced his fair share of therapies over the last three years, since his wife left him and took the kids with her to some other country.

The sea air, the gulls swooping over the dunes and the sound of the waves crashing on the shore made him feel alive again, there was nothing quite like it.

He broke into a slow jog as he neared the Newton

dunes and splashed through the shallows of the outgoing tide. He tried to keep his breathing to a strict rhythm and focused on his shadow ahead of him to block everything else out of his head.

His shadow skimmed across the fine, golden sand and began to undulate as he reached the rock outcrop before the dunes. Then he stopped suddenly, catching his breath and staring at the large sheet of plastic that was partially buried in the sand.

7

After trying to process all the information from the first allegation, and a bit of a chinwag with Dai over a mug of coffee, I got stuck into Vic again.

He sipped his bottled water through smoke-stained teeth and thought for a moment before he spoke. That surprised me because I had no idea he could think. "Right, the second time was around 2005," he finally said. "Me and Sams decided to get out of the valley and set up down in Porthcawl again. We had a van for the season..."

"A van for all seasons?" I cracked, but his puzzled expression proved it was lost on Victor.

"We were 'doing a bit', but travelling out of South Wales and knocking all the gear out over the bridge, just coming back with the cash. Things were going great until one day, we were on the piss in the Dirty Duck, when who comes in?" He nodded and grinned as if I was psychic. "You got it," he continued, "it's Coulter. He scans the bar area and then sees the both of us sat in the corner. Over he comes, the arrogant twat. 'How are things, boys, been out long?' Didn't even give him the time of day, finished our pints, got up, and started to walk.

"We hadn't even got to the bar door when he shouted, 'Hey, boys!' We knew it meant trouble. I looked around and he pointed at us, finger and thumb cocked. 'I'm watching you,' he said to us." Victor mimicked the motion with his own hand.

"We walked back to the van. I was spitting bullets. It was just our luck to have that twat giving us a hard time. Anyway, for the next three or four weeks, Sams and me cooled it a bit and kept a low profile.

"We had a long chat about what to do, knowing that Coulter was on the patch, he was a real spanner in the works. Then, one night, we're having a pint when Elwyn Fowler – you know Elwyn? Likes to think he's fucking Pablo Escobar?"

I shrugged my shoulders and shook my head, but the name did ring a bell.

"Anyway," Vic said, "Elwyn approaches us and starts propositioning us about drugs and how easy it is to make a shed-load of money.

"Some gobby shite had told him we had connections over the bridge and he thought he could... erm... let's say... exploit our entrepreneurial expertise..."

I struggled not to laugh at that one.

"He wanted us to start supplying. Sounded okay, no more screwing houses, we thought. All we had to do was get the connections, Elwyn supplies us and then we knock it out over the bridge for cash and have twenty-five per cent of the take. The go-between would be one of Elwyn's crew, a guy called Lloyd Cove. He lived on the site and was well-known to everyone.

"Everything was going great for a few months. Me and Sams were pulling about two grand a week, happy days!

"Then, one night, Lloyd called around with a kilo of speed and told us to deliver it the following morning. So, we hid it in an empty Calor gas bottle that had a false bottom that Lloyd kindly provided," he said with sarcasm. "After Lloyd left, me and Sams just crashed. We were due to leave early for Bristol to knock out the speed. But all that went tits-up a few hours later. The caravan door came crashing in, two hooded Rambos, screaming and carrying machine guns. 'Get down on the floor, hands behind your heads,' and all that Miami Vice malarkey. We shit ourselves.

"The next bloke we see is that twat Coulter. 'How are you, boys? You're under arrest for supplying', he says. 'Fuck off,' I say back to him. 'We ain't got fuck all.' The bastard smiled at us. 'Haven't you?' he says. He goes straight to the Calor gas bottle and pulls out the kilo. 'Naughty, naughty,' he says. Sams looks at me and says, 'Oh fuck, not again.' Anyway, to cut this next bit a little shorter, they cart us off, top and tail us and that's another two years down the river. We were set up again, honour among thieves? What a load of bollocks!"

I was exhausted just listening to all that. "Fair play, Vic," I said. "Looks like you never learn. Is that all you've got on Coulter?"

"Fuck me, Ter, ain't that enough for you?"

I could see his point.

"Tell me about this rape... what's that all about?"

He nodded. "I had this info from a bloke I was in the nick with – the last time around. We was sharing a cell. Phil Asher, he was. Bloke's a pimp. Black as the ace of spades. Did all his business down the docks. Started young, like most of the girls he had down there. Anyway, we got talking and Coulter's name cropped up and he just blurted it out. He said that Coulter raped and beat up one of his girls, years ago. Threatened her that if she reported it, he would have her sorted. Apparently, she did report it, but told the police she didn't know who the bloke was. They did all the business on her; you know, photographs, DNA, semen, the lot. She picked up a few quid off the Criminal Injuries and let it go."

"Do you know the girl's name?"

"No, can't help you there, but there should be a record."

"So that's it, Vic? Sounds like a load of shit to me. What you making all this up for?"

He looked affronted. "Listen now, Ter, this is all straight up. Why make it up? Me and Sams are getting on now, the less dealings we have with you lot the better. We thought hard about this. We were going to let it slide but then I saw Coulter on the sodding news talking about crime reduction and stuff. That really got me steaming. When I told Sams that I wanted to dob Coulter in it, he said you'd be the boy to talk to. Must admit that I thought you'd believe us. We trust you, even though you're a pig."

He sat back in his chair and folded his arms. "If you want this piece of shit to get away with it, carry on, but it'll be on your conscience."

Now *I* was affronted. "You cheeky twat! Conscience? What do you know about that? Surprised you can even pronounce it."

He shrugged.

"Listen," I said. "I'll investigate it. I just hope Sams' statement corroborates yours."

"It will, Ter, believe me, it will."

The interview was then terminated, and John brought Sams in to join us. I promised them both I'd do my best and they took off in Vic's grandmother's BMW. But, as that old saying goes, 'the best laid plans of mice and men'... and all that bollocks and I was just about to get news of one very big spanner that was about to be dropped into the works.

8

November was never a good month for clement weather in Wales and this one was no exception. A cold mist seemed to permeate every stitch of my clothing, right through to my soul. The streets hadn't had a chance to dry for weeks, my head still pounded from the after-effects of that bottle of red wine the night before and my mood matched the weather as I answered the call. I hadn't even had a chance to speak to John about his interview with Sams.

"Just to let you know, boss. There's a body been found down Newton Dunes, not far from the gravel pits and the car park."

"Be there in ten," I grumbled. I really didn't need any more grief.

I finished my rapidly cooling cup of black coffee and sat back in my chair for a moment. My office was small and full of crap. Tan and brown folders were stacked by the dozen on my desk and also in teetering piles on the floor around every wall. I promised myself that I'd sort the place out one day but to be honest I knew I was lying to myself. Truth was, I was always happiest amongst a mess. I never could do tidy. My mind was somehow more organised when in the centre of chaos.

I dropped the plastic cup of coffee dregs into an already full wastebasket and watched as it bounced off an empty pizza box, which had been discarded days earlier, and fall to the carpet-tiled floor. I ignored the cup and stretched my arm in the opposite direction to pull my jacket from the coat stand my wife bought me a year ago after she had got fed up with ironing my suits. I slipped my arms inside my coat, remaining seated.

I sighed and thought about Molly and wondered what I should do for our anniversary. Twenty-six years wasn't a special anniversary in the grand scheme of things but it was pretty special for us, considering what Molly had put up with over the years. I had to get her something special. The Celtic Manor Resort came to mind. We had been there once before; I enjoyed a round of golf whilst Molly pampered herself in the spa. I thought about a meal and a stay-over. I pulled the desk drawer open and looked at the open bank statement sitting at the top of yet more files. I squinted at the balance on our accounts. The Celtic Manor wasn't going to be an option after all.

I drove my pool-car, a three-year-old Ford Focus, down to Newton, a small, quiet village in itself but which is adjacent to the biggest and liveliest caravan site in Europe. It's a pretty place, if you ignore the inevitable crap that springs up around any holiday attraction.

Two PCs from Traffic were waiting for me and they loaded me in to the back of their marked car and drove me across the dunes in their nice clean BMW 4x4. The grey sky was obviously no fan of traffic coppers and dumped a torrent of rain that quickly made a mess of their shiny car. I couldn't help grinning from my back seat at the moans from the 'black rats' up front.

Five minutes of bouncing around – like one of the Coney Beach rides – got me to the scene. They were all there, the whole shooting match. scenes of crime officer, the police surgeon, a couple of community support officers and even the uniform superintendent – mind you, why he was there I had no idea. He was a Bramshill boy, waste of space, wouldn't know a murder from a double-yellow line.

"What have we got?" I asked of anyone who could provide an answer.

The SOCO – an old boy of twenty-five years' service – was dressed in a white coverall that was straining against the zip at his waist and doing his best to look efficient. "Male, early thirties, blond hair... hippy looking... oh aye, got a few track marks. He's been wrapped up in polythene, done up tight as a drum. Obviously been buried, but not deep enough. The tide has done the business for us."

"Who found it?"

"Some bloke taking a jog this morning. One of the uniforms is taking a statement from him."

The police surgeon was reading the SOCO's notes and keeping a wary eye on me. He knew me too well.

"What do you think, Doc?"

Doctor Hugo Faulkner clucked his tongue and handed the notes back to the old sweat. "Hard to say, Terry. He's well-preserved. I think he's been there for a while."

I was intrigued... and confused. "How could it be well-preserved after being dead for some time? It's common knowledge, even for someone like the superintendent there, that bodies decay," I said as I watched the superintendent scowl at me. "Seems we have a contradiction, unless we have Tutan-fucking-Khamun?" I watched the superintendent shake his head in disapproval of my use of the expletive but he said nothing – the man had no balls!

"Bag it and tag it, then down to the morgue so we can get a better look. We'll know more after the PM," I said.

Crooked DI Coulter would probably have to go on the back burner for a while.

9

To the morgue I went. It was a whitewashed brick shithouse of a place at the back of the local hospital that reeked of disinfectant. A tall, white chimney rose thirty feet into the air above the morgue and although I knew its purpose I didn't really want to think about its use.

I conferred with old Professor Powell. Although I knew he was officially called 'Professor' in his profession I had always called him Doc and he had never seemed to mind. He was a cracking bloke. He had been the Home Office pathologist so long I swear he'd performed the autopsy on the Cain and Abel murder case. Never seen anyone like him when it came to using a scalpel and a saw: he was a true artist at work.

We had a bit of a con-flab, prior to the slicing and dicing, and then it was down to business.

Now, I have never been any good at the old post-mortem. In fact, I'd always found that clean, clinical smell a little unnerving, especially when there was a body on the slab and other odours began to permeate the room. To keep things on an even keel for me, I dipped my finger into a large pot of Vicks petroleum jelly on a shelf near the door and smeared some of it around my nose.

The polythene, nylon rope and all the clothing from the victim had already been removed by the SOC officer and were on the way to the lab.

The Professor then began his work. First order of business for him was always a cursory examination. "Definitely got a murder here, Terry, my old son."

"No shit, Sherlock."

Powell raised one brow and snorted. "Look at the chest. At least three stab wounds. Up close and personal, I would say."

"Hardly going to be a long-distance stabbing, now is it?" I cracked.

This comment got a two-eyebrow raise from the Prof. "Are you going to be a smart-arse all the way through the examination or just for this bit?"

I held up my hands in surrender.

"I'll know more after I've opened him up," the Professor continued. "I'll do a full toxicology report as well, bearing in mind the track marks. A *big* user, I would say."

"Any idea of time of death, Doc?"

He nodded his head slowly but his expression suggested he wasn't certain. "This bloke's been put on ice. I reckon... somewhere like... five to ten..."

"Days?"

He shook his head. "Oh no. I'd say five to ten *years*."

I did a double-take, like Daffy Duck. "Fuck me, Doc. Are you catching a dose of smart-arse, too? You're telling me that he's been stabbed three times and then kept refrigerated for years like a bag of frozen peas?"

Powell nodded more confidently now.

I scratched my head. "Fuck me, that's a first."

10

Early evening in the CID office at the Bridgend nick was nothing like it used to be a decade ago. Structurally it was the same, but the atmosphere had changed. It no longer felt like the station I once saw as a second home. The office wasn't particularly large. There was enough space for eight desks with computers on each on the third floor of the old red brick Victorian or Edwardian building. To be honest, I didn't have a clue about architecture classifications but I knew the station had been there for decades before I was born. My dad had worked out of there. He'd taken me to the station a few times when I was a kid but had told me firmly that I was never to follow him into the police force. Dad had died a short while before I joined the Force, killed on duty, and it was his death that spurred me on to join up. It was a decision I had never once truly regretted.

At one time the station was a busy place but had officially been closed for some years since the introduction of the purpose-built Bridewell Custody Centre, on an industrial estate on the outskirts of the town. Now the station was only used for incidents, such as murder enquiries. In the old days there would be detectives compiling files of evidence or typing up statements from notebooks. Others would be out on enquiries. But there would usually be at least one detective in the CID office to field the calls unless there was a major incident to deal with, and then the office would be stuffed to capacity until they were given their orders. It was sad to see the old place neglected but I also understood the financial constraints on the service that were crippling real policing.

I had called my team together for a briefing. Two of my younger detectives were off on courses, one a firearms course and the other in Liverpool on a basic detective course, so I knew we'd be depleted as a team.

The smell from the coffee machine filled the briefing room as I strolled in to speak to those assembled. It was only a small team, DS Dai Williams, three DC's, a uniform inspector and the Collator from downstairs.

"Right, ladies and gentleman," I said, "this is what we've got. A male body in a bag, buried in the dunes near the gravel pits. Stabbed three times in the chest. However, I don't think he was killed there." I stopped nd looked at my team scribbling notes in their books. "Why is our glorious leader thinking this, I hear you ask? I'll tell you why. It looks as if he was kept on ice for at least five to ten years before he was buried, and no, I don't want any *Frozen* jokes."

Roger Bailey, a ginger-haired young DC, a smart-arse with a quick wit, couldn't miss the opportunity. "I think we should just *let it go*, boss."

I stifled a grin, not wanting to encourage him. "It looks like this bloke was a serious user, too. So, I want you to get out there, speak to your narks, and let's find

46

out who this guy is. I'll have more info tomorrow after the results from the lab and PM. As from now, this is a murder enquiry. This guy must have been missed over the years... surely? There must be a MISPER report on file somewhere. I hope tomorrow will make things a little clearer."

As I was about to leave the briefing, a young uniform policewoman entered, looking very sheepish. "Er, sir," she said.

I forced a weary smile to try and make her feel at ease as all eyes turned towards her. I never forgot what it was like speaking to brass when I was a sprog. "What can I do you for, young lady?" I said as I beckoned her to follow me into my office.

She smiled, bright white teeth almost blinded me. "I know you're up to your eyes in things, but I've just had a report on the desk that we've got a flasher down on Trecco Bay Caravan Park. There's been two incidents down there now."

I tried to hide my annoyance. There's an old saying I always kept in my mind: don't shoot the messenger. "Okay," I said. "Isn't there anyone in uniform who can deal with it?"

The young woman looked embarrassed. "Sorry, sir. The sergeant got me to log it on the system but the Super walked in as I was telling him about it and said I should come and tell you."

I nodded. The uniform superintendent at the station and I had never seen eye to eye. He knew I disliked 'Bramshill Flyers' and he was always looking for ways to add more grief to my day and probably still had the hump from my insults earlier at the beach.

"I'm up to my eyes in this body on the beach," I explained. "Could you do me a big favour and go and take the report and the witness statements? I'll get a DC onto it as soon as one is free."

"Yes, sir."

The policewoman slipped from the room and I was left thinking of another saying: when it rains it pours.

11

Detective work always has to be focussed. Briefings help everyone to understand what's going on and that's the reason we always seem to have lots of them. I had called another briefing the next day and knew this one would at least provide some more tangible information for us to work with.

"Settle down, ladies and gents," I said to the team assembled before me again. I knew my main speaker at the briefing was well known to most present but I also knew young Bailey had never met him before. I did an official introduction for Bailey's benefit. "I would like to introduce you to Home Office Pathologist, Professor Bernard Powell. Professor Powell will fill us all in on the post-mortem results, cause of death, etc." I sat on a chair off to the side for the good doctor to glory in the limelight.

"Well, first off the bat... the cause of death was multiple stab wounds to the chest, three to be precise, severing the aorta and puncturing the heart twice. The only other injury was to the victim's face, he'd been battered post-mortem, you'd be hard-pressed to recognise him. In my opinion the murder weapon was a double-serrated blade about six inches long. Time of death?" The doctor looked up at his audience, as if someone had asked the question. "I would estimate time of death to be about five years ago," he watched the stunned expressions on the faces of the team before continuing. "The body has been well-preserved by freezing and probably only recently been moved to where it was discovered." He scanned his notes. "As for toxicology, there's nothing. However, there is no doubt that this man was an intravenous drug user, judging by the needle-track marks."

He took a sip from a plastic cup of coffee and wiped a spill from his Paisley-patterned tie and tan corduroy jacket before continuing: "No defensive wounds. Like I said, up close and personal. As far as dental identification is concerned, I have never seen a mouth in such bad condition, looks like that guy who sings for the Pogues. No fillings, indeed, no dental work at all. In fact, he had a mouth like a sewer. I don't think there is anything else I can add that will be of evidential value..." He turned a page in his notes and flipped back to the cover sheet and held up his hand as if asking for permission to continue, "Oh sorry, did I mention all his fingertips had been burnt away? By acid."

The doctor waited for questions.

I remained seated. "What about age?"

"Early thirties, Terry, I would guess."

"Any other questions?" I asked the others.

The room remained silent, so I stood. "At least now we have a bit of a profile to work with."

DS Glyn Walcott stepped forward from the front row of seats and the pathologist ducked into Glyn's vacated chair.

Glyn was a seasoned scenes of crime officer and was nearing retirement. He'd worked on many murders across the Force and it would be fair to say that Glyn was meticulous to the point of tedium. Even his face matched his personality – serious, meticulously shaved, thinning grey hair slicked back into a style that reminded me of Phil Collins during his major hair-loss phase. He had begun to put on a bit of timber around the waist but I'd seen far worse on others of his advancing age.

"What have you got for us, Glyn?" I said.

He cleared his throat. "This is it, in a nutshell, boss. The polythene is industrial, mass-produced, normally used in caravan manufacturing and it's been cut with a serrated knife. As far as clothing goes, it's quite high-end, all designer stuff; Abercrombie top, Adidas bottoms, and Nike trainers. No pants or socks. No joy on the fingerprints, didn't lift a mark off anything, as for the fingers... it's like the Doc said, all burnt with acid. He had 'Love' and 'Hate' tattooed across both knuckles. As you know only too well, that's quite common. I don't think we can help any further at this time."

"So, someone had wanted to hide the victim's identity. But why?" I said as I looked around the team.

"The only reason I can think of is that the identity could connect the victim to the killer or killers," Roger Bailey offered.

I nodded. He was beginning to think like me.

12

Good police work sometimes depends upon stating the bleeding obvious and repeating it until it stuck and triggered something in someone, somewhere. So, I never broke that habit and always kept reminding everyone of the facts we had. That's why I believed in frequent briefings. I'd listened to the briefing from Doc Powell and from Glyn and was keen to dig a little deeper.

"Right, this is what we've got so far. Time of death about five years ago, so we'll say... take it to be from January 1st, 2011. We have a white male, aged thirty to thirty-five years, blond hair, intravenous drug user, wore high-end clothing, but didn't take care of himself... possibly had some form, going by the tattoos or he had them done to make others believe he had some form. We struck out on fingerprint and dental identification. Bearing in mind the proximity of where the body was discovered to the caravan site and the polythene, is there a connection there we can follow?

"I've been reliably informed that the plastic is similar to the stuff used to cover furniture and might have come from one of the new caravans or perhaps a new car?"

"The sheet's too big to be from car seats, boss," Glyn Walcott chipped in. "I'd put my money on a caravan or perhaps someone's settee or bed or something."

"Thank you, Glyn. As for the freezing? Well, that

could have been done anywhere." I paused and called to Dai. "Sort out the teams: house-to-house, missing persons, you know the drill. Next briefing at the same time tomorrow, unless something turns up before."

We were now thirty-six hours into the enquiry and I had nothing to show for it, not even a clue as to who the poor bastard was. I felt I could do with a swift half. Was the victim just a user, or a supplier? Someone, somewhere must have missed him? Was he a fairground worker, a transient from the valleys? Why kill a bloke, batter him, freeze him, then bury him years later? Didn't make sense.

I needed to find out more about someone who was a regular drug user, his habit, where he'd get the gear from, how often and if any of our own officers might know of someone like that who had suddenly disappeared five years ago. I had known many druggies during my career but knew things changed all the time. New drugs, users and dealers came to prominence all the time and I was acutely aware that I couldn't afford to be complacent. Ten years ago, when I dealt with lots of drug offenders, I'd probably have been better prepared, but I rang a mate of mine on the Drug Squad, Cliff Ambrose. Cliff started in the job with me over twenty years before. He flew up through the ranks pretty quickly and had become a DCI. Knowing the victim's drug history I thought a chat with the DCI of the Drug Squad would be a smart move.

"Hi, Cliff, how are you doing?" I didn't wait for a

reply. "I've got a real ripper on at the moment, butt. Bloke found buried down the gravels in Newton, stabbed repeatedly. Been kept on ice for a few years by the looks of it. Think he may have been involved in drugs but we can't identify him."

Cliff's gruff voice, from a lifetime of smoking thirty Regals a day until he became a born-again non-smoker, grunted down the line. "How can I help?"

"I wonder if you could have a word with the squad?" I continued. "Particularly the old sweats. You never know what might pop up. I'm talking about a bloke who might have disappeared off the face of the earth around five years ago."

"Five years?"

"Seems so. Someone must have a big freezer."

"That's a new one on me."

"Me too," I admitted.

"I'll have a word with the lads. See if someone slipped off the radar about that time."

"Be good for us if one of your lads could speak to one of mine, DC Roger Bailey, and give him some background on the day-in-the-life type of stuff."

I was confident that Cliff's boys would know anyone local who met the criteria. Knowing the users was always good for getting to know the dealers. The detectives working with the users and dealers always made me uncomfortable. They looked so much like the lowlife they were dealing with on a daily basis and I often wondered if any of them dabbled in a little illicit substance on the side. I hoped not but understood human nature better than most. I had heard stories of officers in some places taking drugs to build their undercover identities. I just couldn't imagine how anyone could do that. Was that dedication to the job or plain stupidity? Who was I to judge? They had their ways of working and I had mine. I got a buzz out of solving cases but I had a feeling that this murder was going to be tricky. We had already lost five years since he was killed and that meant the killer or killers had had five years to make good their escape.

13

Extended investigations were always bad news. It was week six of the frozen body murder and, because of budget constraints plus all the other bureaucracy we had to deal with on a daily basis, I had reluctantly been forced to trim the team down to the bare bones. One of my lads had been taken off me to look into the 'Dick of the Dunes' case, as the flasher had become known within the station. Only Dai and the cocky DC Bailey were doing anything with the murder. Roger Bailey had spent a few hours with the Drug Squad but had not been impressed with their reluctance to talk. He had been told nothing more than he already knew. The team kept me updated on a daily basis. I knew Dai was frustrated because all our leads had turned to rat shit. We were no nearer to identifying the poor sod who died than we were at the outset, let alone catching the bastard who killed him.

Since the murder enquiry had gone a bit tits-up, I asked John Fuller to meet up to listen to the taped interviews of Vic and his pal, Sams, over and over again. I eased the boredom with an occasional glass of malt. John had returned to the Special Branch for a few weeks after I put the Coulter enquiry temporarily to bed to deal with the iceman murder. Now things were up and running again on the corruption enquiry.

"What do you reckon, John, do you think they're on the level?"

"Well, put it this way, what they say about the two fit-ups is very plausible. I know Coulter's reputation went before him. His nickname was 'The Fox', probably because he's a sly bastard alright. As for the rape? Well, I'm not convinced. We only have Thomas's take on that."

"To be honest, John, and I rarely stick my neck out, but I think it's all genuine. I want you to trace where this bloke, Diamond, is doing his bird and fix up a visit. He's a lifer, so he may give us Coulter on a platter. This guy called Lloyd Cove? Trace him. Let's see what his take is on the drugs. Thirdly, there's the rape. See if it was reported and try to find out who the girl is. I'll update the ACC in the morning... enough for one day. I think I'll do something unusual - I'm going to go home early. See you tomorrow."

* * *

"So what are you doing about the reduction in police numbers?" Councillor Chris Coulter demanded to know.

"You know we are tied by ever tightening budgets, Mr Coulter," the Crime Commissioner for the South Wales Police said. "You, of all people in this room, know exactly what we have had to work with over the last few years."

Chris Coulter frowned. "Yes, I know, but surely we could redirect the funding from the PCSO's and back into regular police officers? Why on earth are we paying so much for officers who are restricted in their duties, who are unable to do the work a regular officer can whilst the numbers of regular officers have dropped to a point where they are unable to do their jobs properly?"

The Crime Commissioner, a Labour Party appointee who had been parachuted into the job and elected on her previous reputation as a Member of Parliament, nodded her head. "I agree with you to some extent but I would have to defend the PCSOs. They are doing what they can and doing it well. I accept your concerns but we have to be sensible and cut our cloth according to its width."

Coulter drove directly home from the meeting. It had lasted less than an hour but he had signed in and would be paid well for his membership of the committee. Being a county councillor certainly had its perks. He walked into his kitchen and opened a twelve-pound bottle of Merlot he had had delivered as one of twelve he received free each week for 'entertaining dignitaries'.

The wine was not the best he had tasted, but it would do.

He sat at his dining table and logged into his online banking app. He smiled at the three thousand pounds in one of his accounts. It didn't seem like much to others, perhaps, but he had to keep his official accounts within expectations for a man in his position. He was divorced and had paid a huge sum to his ex-wife. If the cash he had at home appeared in his bank account, then questions would be asked. Life since retirement from the police had been interesting.

His phone began to vibrate in his hand. He checked the caller ID. "What can I do for you," he asked the caller.

"We might have a problem," the caller said.

14

John had traced Steve Diamond to HMP Dartmoor and I knew we had to get everything out of him if the enquiry was to move forward. I'd left the murder enquiry ticking over gently in the capable hands of Dai and felt it was only right that I accompanied John to speak to Diamond – if the bastard was willing to talk to us.

First thing on our agenda was to speak to the Governor, in order to find out if Diamond would give us the time of day. There was no point in travelling all the way there to find out that he wouldn't even speak to us. After some time on hold, we had the nod from the Governor and I arranged the visit. He was good as gold and reminded us to bring a stock of smokes for the prisoner.

I was hoping that Diamond would come up trumps for us – excuse the pun. I needed Diamond preferably to negate Vic and Sams' claims, or to confirm them. If I could get him to confirm the story I'd heard so far I'd be more confident taking the case forward. If not, we were just left with unsubstantiated allegations from two well-known criminals.

We set off early for the long trip to Dartmoor and made our way east through the busy morning traffic along the M4 and then on the M5 south to Exeter and the B3357 on the Tavistock road. We eventually got to the prison about ten in the morning. The mist was low across the moor. The rain had been intermittent all the way but had now increased in intensity and was bouncing off the bonnet of the car when I saw the grey brick monolith of a building. It was honestly like a scene from the *Hound of the Baskervilles* and it didn't matter how many times I'd seen it, I always got the same impression, even on sunny days.

We pulled off the road and entered through the various layers of security to meet the Governor. I was impressed that he actually showed us to the interview room himself. He was very obliging. "Anything you need, just speak to the boys. I've told them to look after you and help you any way they can." He turned and ordered one of his staff to go and get Diamond for us.

John and I took the weight off our feet. The room was quite plush, considering. Easy chairs and lovely, clean, freshly painted walls made me think it looked like the lounge of an old people's home rather than a prison.

"Nice and relaxing, butt. Hope this twat plays ball," I said, just as Diamond walked in. I must admit that I was expecting a big strapper, but this bloke was quite small, well-built though, clean-cut, and looked like butter wouldn't melt in his mouth. First impressions could be deceiving, I reminded myself. This bloke was a killer.

"How are you, Steve?" My opening gambit. "I'm DI McGuire and this is DC Fuller, but you can call us Terry and John."

He sat opposite us, with an odd expression on his face, one I couldn't read. It was as if he'd seen a ghost.

"No sweat," he replied. "Bring any fags?"

John tossed forty Benson on to the table. The warden gave me the nod and I lit one up for Diamond. He savoured the smoke, took a big drag, his less than impressive chest puffed out, then he let the smoke go slowly into the air, clearly relishing the toxic shit as the room was filled with that horrible, acrid stench.

"What can I do for you, boys? Must be important for a DI to come all this way."

Sharp twat! I thought.

"What can you tell me about two chancers – Vic Thomas and his mate, Samuels?"

He took another big drag, exhaled and said with a grin, "Those two fucking muppets? Haven't seen them for years."

I go in for the kill. "What about Chris Coulter?"

His whole demeanour changed, he stubbed the cigarette out and put his hand over his mouth, rubbing at his face.

"What do you want to know?"

"What can you tell me about him?" I thought he looked worried.

"Did he send you?"

"Why would you think that?"

"He didn't, did he?" he grinned. "Must be something serious for you to want to speak to me about one of your own."

"He's not one of us." I told him emphatically. "You might have heard that Coulter has retired?" I looked at

Diamond, but if he had heard he certainly wasn't giving anything away. "Vic Thomas and Samuels are alleging he fitted them up for a job in Porthcawl a few years ago and that you were involved."

He thought for a minute. "What's in it for me?"

I shrugged my shoulders. "Depends what you've got to say."

"And I'm to trust you on that, eh?" He smiled.

"What have you got to lose?"

He asked me to light another cigarette and I was beginning to feel sick from the taste.

"Okay. Yes, I was narking for him at one time, but we fell out over my money. He was getting more than me, I took all the risks, and he was getting the glory. Wasn't just the icing, it was two-thirds of the fucking cake, too."

"Go on..."

"That's all I want to say. When I got in the shit with the murder, he dropped me like a hot potato."

"Look, Steve. You've got fuck all to lose, butt. Give me something on the bastard."

"Then tell me, what's in it for me? All I want is to be closer to home. Not a lot to ask, is it?"

John shook his head but remained silent.

"I can't promise you anything," I answered truthfully, "but you never know. If I can nail Coulter and send him down... I'll do what I can."

That seemed to be enough for him.

"Coulter wanted me to set up a job, involving

firearms, not a robbery, just a burglary where guns would be found.

"I knew Thomas and Samuels were at it in Porthcawl, so I propositioned them about doing the bookies on the Esplanade."

"Did they know about the guns?"

"Fuck no. Coulter got them for me, from where I don't know, but they were the real McCoy, no numbers on them, clean as whistles."

"Go on."

"Well, I showed the retards the guns and they fucking handled them, that's all Coulter wanted, their dabs on the guns. We did the job, I planted the guns, they got caught, I got away. Simple, innit? Coulter gets a high-profile firearms case and I get a few quid."

It was exactly as Vic and Sams had said.

"Is there anything else you can help us with?"

"You pot Coulter then come back and see me, Ter, your head will spin, but that should be enough for now."

"So, what Vic and Sams are alleging is true?"

"Yes, straight from the horses, boys."

"Will you make a statement and give evidence?"

He thought for a moment then nodded his head. "Fuck, why not? The poor fuckers had a fiver, didn't they? And Coulter didn't bat a fucking eyelid."

I left John to take the statement, which was now the first nail in the coffin of Chris Coulter.

We finished up at the prison and set off for the long journey home.

15

John had been through the archives and, lo and behold, a rape had been reported down the Bay in Cardiff around the time Victor Thomas alleged.

We went through the file together. The girl involved was Mandy Keller; she was only eighteen at the time, with the same sad, stereotypical background I'd seen so many times before. Brought up with an abusive father, alcoholic mother, in and out of care, eventually ending up on the streets around the Bay. What else could she do? Born into a dysfunctional family, the hand she had been dealt was loaded against her from the start. Who was I to judge?

All the exhibits were still stored and the DNA evidence was still on file. The photographs were quite explicit: the girl had been given a good beating, no doubt about that.

The next job was to trace her and, hopefully, she'd be the second nail in Coulter's coffin.

Within the hour, John had got an address for the girl, but it was only a 'last known'.

Because we were on a roll, we made our way to the Bay as soon as we got the address. The place had changed out of all recognition. High-rise apartments had sprung up all around the old docks and the whole place had been transformed from a drab, grey industrial landscape to an affluent residential paradise for those who could afford it. It was a far cry from the days when prostitutes toured the streets in search of a seedy buck and drunken, horny seamen were rolling out of all the local pubs and looking to take advantage of the delights on offer.

We arrived at the address in Loudon Place and knocked the door to be greeted by an elderly Indian lady.

"I'm trying to trace Mandy Keller. Does she live here?" I asked.

She shook her head.

"Do you know her?"

She nodded. We might be in luck, I thought.

"Yes," she said, "but she doesn't live here anymore, she used to lodge with me."

My optimism began to fade. "Do you know where she lives now?"

She nodded again.

"Yes, she's married now and lives in Ninian Road, must be for some fifteen years."

"And her married name?"

"Jordon, Mandy Jordon."

It was the result I had hoped for.

I smiled warmly. "Thank you very much."

Me and John got back to the car to ponder for a moment. I knew we were thinking the same thing. Were we going to open old scars for this woman?

We called in a quick voter check and got the address over my phone and we were there at Mandy's new address in ten minutes.

I knocked the door to be greeted by a small,

attractive blonde woman, I introduced ourselves and she invited us in. The house was well maintained, beautifully decorated and a sweet smell of incense permeated the air. We sat down, I took a deep breath and I explained the reason we'd called.

"Do you remember a copper called Chris Coulter, Amanda?"

Her eyes searched the floor and seemed reluctant to return to meet mine. "Oh yes," she said through gritted teeth. "I will never forget that man, he's evil."

"So I've been led to believe," I assured her. I wanted her to know from the outset that I was on her side.

She looked me in the eyes. "He raped me when I was eighteen."

I was a little bit taken aback by her blunt statement and I think I flinched. I wondered if I should have brought a policewoman with us but there hadn't been one in the office when we left and I honestly didn't think we'd find Amanda. I thought she might have wanted to forget about the assault and deny it. I still had to give her the option of a female presence, even if that meant leaving and returning later.

"Would you be more comfortable with a female officer?" I asked.

She shook her head forcefully. "No, it's okay. I did complain about the rape at the time, but he threatened me, so when I went to the nick to report it, the only thing I didn't tell the police was Coulter's identity. I told them it was a first-time client."

"How did it happen, Amanda?"

"He was a young plain-clothes officer. All the girls thought he was handsome, and he was a flirt. One night, I bumped into him down by The Packet pub and he propositioned me. I didn't want anything to do with him, I had to be careful because of my pimp, Phil Asher. He used to watch me like a hawk. I said I wasn't interested, but Coulter wouldn't take no for an answer and dragged me across the road to a big doorway in Bute Crescent, beat me about the head and raped me there in the doorway. I was bleeding and crying. The bastard broke my jaw. I couldn't move, it was the first time anyone had beat me since my father."

I knew The Packet pub well. It was a stark architectural contrast to the sleek modern redevelopment of the Bay area. It stood on the corner of Bute Street and New George Street. The three-storey pub boasted grand stone window reveals on the ground floor with square leaded windows. The sign hanging above the entrance showed a clipper in full sail, a reminder of its maritime history. Even though the area had undergone a rebuild over the years, the pub was as popular as it had ever been.

"He just left me and told me if I reported it, he would kill me. I was terrified and managed to crawl back to The Packet, where Phil was drinking.

"I told Phil what had happened. He put me in the car and took me to the Central Police Station to report it. I told him what Coulter had threatened and he said,

'Tell them everything as it was but say you didn't recognise the bloke. There's a few grand in compensation in this, but don't you dare mention Coulter's name, I'll sort him.'"

"So, that's what I did. The officers were very nice. I was examined and photographed, but nothing ever came of it. I think they just went through the motions."

"We still have all the original statements. Will you give us an additional one?" John asked.

She brightened, possibly envisioning a revenge she must have thought would never come. "Yes, of course. Will he go to prison?"

"I hope so, Amanda," I said, in all honesty.

A tall, smart bloke in a pin-stripe suit walked into the lounge. I guessed it was Amanda's husband.

"It's okay," she said, "he knows everything."

She told him why we were there, and he shook our hands and gave Amanda a big cwtsh. She cried into his shoulder.

After a few minutes, Amanda regained composure and I wanted to know why she had stayed in the same area and not taken off somewhere else?

"It was a long time ago and Coulter never bothered me again. I knew he could find me wherever I went so what was the point in running? Anyway, when he realised I hadn't mentioned his name, he seemed to be happy to leave me alone. I didn't think he'd kill me or anything. He was a coward. He was a bully but I wasn't enough of a threat to him for him to kill me. I heard he was moved shortly after and then I met my husband and moved too. I didn't think he'd know about that and certainly not know my married name."

Made sense.

John took a short statement and I chipped in with some questions I thought needed to be answered for the statement. Amanda was thorough and I felt sorry for stirring up the terrible events of her past but it was essential if I wanted to put Coulter behind bars.

We finally left them to get on with their lives.

I sat in the car and thought about Amanda and her husband. My intuition told me that her husband used to be a client of hers and that he had probably rescued her from the streets. Not quite a real version of *Pretty Woman*, but close enough for me. I liked happy endings. At least she would have closure, if I could put Coulter away.

Nail two in his coffin.

16

I was sitting in the office with a small glass of malt. My head was spinning, not from the whisky but because there was so much going on and not enough hours in a day, juggling enquiries, home life a rare pleasure. I often wondered why I put myself and my family through it all. There again, it was my life, it was what I was good at, the only thing I was ever good at.

To top and tail the rape, I had tasked John to trace the pimp, Phil Asher. I didn't tell Amanda we'd be contacting him and I didn't want Asher contacting her. To be fair who would want a twat like that back in your life, sleeping dogs, and all that. She could do without me resurrecting him. I had my first chat with the ACC and brought him up to speed with the enquiry. He was more than happy with the way it was progressing.

John traced Asher to a bail hostel in Cardiff, a sixties monstrosity of modernist architectural insanity. The hostel occupied the ground floor of the grey concrete box. Large glass panes filled one wall of the building and full-length net drapes were permanently drawn for privacy. Asher had just come out of prison after doing yet another stretch, this time for drugs, how unusual. Anyway, the interview with him in a room with one of the net drapes confirmed Amanda's story, and the kicker he added was that Coulter was also on the take, putting the arm on the pimps, Asher being one of them.

John told Asher he wanted to tie him down to specifics. "Did you ever take Coulter to task over the rape of Amanda?" He asked him and made a note of his reply. I sat silently, not wanting to break John's stride.

"Of course not. I told her I would take care of him, but hey, you could tell her anything. I didn't challenge Coulter, he was a loose cannon, he'd have had me topped. No, Amanda had two-and-a-half-grand compo, I kept about eighteen hundred, gave her two and Coulter five."

It was hard to believe, I thought. So, Coulter rapes and beats up an eighteen-year-old prostitute, he's a serving police officer and he gets paid five hundred quid for his trouble. It's not prison he deserved, the twat needed castrating. I also fumed at the fact that the pimp got eighteen-hundred quid and poor Amanda got just two-hundred pounds of the award meant to help her.

"How is Mandy doing these days," he asked with a grin on his face.

"She's made a new life away from you and what you made her do," I said firmly.

He shook his head. "I didn't make her do anything. I just looked after the girls.

Now I grinned but there was no humour intended. "Let me tell you now. If you ever bump into her again I want you to ignore her as if you don't remember her and

I want you to walk away without a word. Do you understand what I'm saying?"

He snorted. "And what if I don't?"

"Your life won't be worth living. I'll hound you, I'll be wherever you look. I'll ruin every seedy little thing you do. Or... you can take my advice and we'll stay well clear of each other. So, what's it to be?"

He nodded.

I didn't like Asher. He was arrogant. His prison stays were no issue for him, they were just part and parcel of his life. I simply couldn't understand that mentality.

Still, he had played ball with us over the Coulter business and that was all that mattered to me.

Nail number three for the bastard.

17

We now had the last piece of the jigsaw to find, as far as Coulter was concerned. We had to trace this bloke called Lloyd Cove. Vic and Sams said that he was the go-between regarding the drug supplying and that he brought the kilo of speed to the caravan prior to them getting busted. If we could trace him, that would be it, get him to talk and then we could really go to town on Coulter.

Initial enquiries proved fruitless. Cove had a bit of form, but he appeared to have vanished from the area. John spent hours digging for previous addresses and linking them to possible phone numbers. Each call was fruitless. Then our luck changed.

I knew I had to sniff around Vic and Sams' old hunting ground. Time had passed but there might still be someone living or working in the area who might know of Lloyd Cove. I called for a pint in the Dirty Duck and sat by the bar, just having a chinwag with the licensee. It wasn't actually just a chinwag. I had a reason for the visit that went above and beyond the desire for an alcoholic beverage. The pub sat at the edge of Trecco Bay Caravan Park and had always done a roaring trade from the holidaymakers. The current manager was a jovial chap and well experienced in the trade. Publicans have always been a great source of information for detectives and it was refreshing for me to go back to my roots for an hour.

I was not in the habit of divulging anything about a case to anyone outside of the job, but I knew the licensee, Bill Duggan. He knew most of the local toe-rags and he was a genuinely good egg.

"Heard of Lloyd Cove?" I asked, as I supped on my pint.

"Aye, haven't seen him for years, not a well bloke."

"What do you mean?"

"Last I heard, he was in some drug rehab place over in Weston-super-Mare. But that was a few years ago, probably popped it by now, after all the shit he put in his arms and up his nose."

I thought that was the end of that. Anyway, I finished my pint and went home. Early night for me – eight o'clock, the missus would think I had fallen out with my fictional fancy-piece.

Molly had thrown together a spaghetti bolognaise and lined up a brace of Guinness. We talked about the kids and watched a few box-set episodes of some detective series set in the Shetland Islands and then went to bed together, for a change.

The following morning, I tasked John with locating the rehab place in Weston. It was more or less a shot in the dark, I was expecting bad news.

Then I went up to the ACC for the update.

"How far are we off an arrest, Terry?"

"Well, I can certainly charge him with two, if the CPS goes for it? But I've got one more iron in the fire and my fingers and toes are all crossed."

I told the ACC everything we had and he just sat there and nodded without saying a word.

I made my way back to the office and then John started playing silly buggers. He was grinning like the Cheshire Cat.

"Guess what, boss?"

"What?" I said.

"Have a guess..." he teased.

"Stop messing about, John, tell me, make my day."

He nodded. "Well, I've traced and spoken to Lloyd Cove and he'll play ball. I've made arrangements to see him later this afternoon."

I punched the air. "Ya-fucking-hoo!"

It was a bit early for the malt.

Within the hour we were off and running. The pool car was full of diesel, Mars bars in the glove box and two lattes occupied the cup holders.

We arrived at the St Christopher Alcohol and Drug Rehab Hostel in Weston-super-Mare just after three in the afternoon. It was a large modern building, with all the mod cons. It was primarily a one-storey white-washed U-shaped building with two wings that extended out on either side of an entrance portico, also white-washed. John drove our pool car in between the two wings and parked it on the grey gravel drive, to the right of the portico.

Above the entrance was another smaller level of what looked like extra bedrooms.

The place was very busy, with men of all ages walking around the manicured lawns around the building, heads bowed, not making eye contact with us. It reminded me of a scene from a zombie movie.

We were greeted at the entrance by a long-haired, casually dressed guy who looked like he just stepped out of Woodstock, tattooed from arsehole to breakfast. He even had a tattoo of a spider's web across his face. He looked about sixty, but I could tell he'd been through the mill with the booze and dope and could have been much younger.

"I'm DI McGuire and this is DC Fuller."

"Yes," he said, "I've been expecting you. I'm Lloyd, Lloyd Cove."

"You're not what I expected." I was genuinely shocked.

"No. I've been clean for many a year now," he sighed and opened the door to a garden. "If I hadn't found this place, I'd be dead."

We followed him out into a pretty, enclosed garden as he rolled and lit a cigarette. .

"What can I do for you?"

I nodded to my mucker. "John filled you in on the phone. We're investigating a retired DI, Chris Coulter, for corruption offences and we hope you can help us?"

"I remember him. The Fox we used to call him. A sly bastard. He had narks all over the place, bent as fuck."

"Did you ever do any jobs for him?"

He shook his head. "Not personally, but my mate, Elwyn Fowler, God rest his soul, used to do the business for him."

"Do you remember two blokes living on Trecco,

started as burglars before Elwyn recruited them to deal drugs over the bridge?"

He laughed. "Oh, that pair of idiots? Batman and Robin – the not-so-dynamic duo, Vic and Sams? The Fox wanted them bad, so he did a deal with Elwyn to fit 'em up. One night Elwyn asked me to do a favour for him, I dropped a kilo of speed off to them, the following day they were busted by The Fox."

"Who supplied the drugs, was it Elwyn?"

Lloyd snorted. "Fuck no, Elwyn wouldn't let a kilo go with no return. No, it was The Fox, he supplied the gear."

"Would you go to court and give evidence, Lloyd? I know it's a big ask and I have to warn you, you may get done yourself."

He looked around the beautifully presented garden and inhaled deeply. "You make it sound like you don't really want me to?"

I shook my head and shrugged. "It's awkward for us, but we'll do what has to be done."

"You know, this is all the work of the inmates," Cole said as he nodded towards the gardens. "Look what can be done with a little help, someone to set you straight... know what I mean?"

I nodded. "I'm beginning to understand, Lloyd."

He took another drag from his cigarette. "Listen, I've been here for a few years now, they know my past. I'm clean. I counsel these poor bastards, what mileage is in it for them to prosecute me now? Truth be told, I've got about a twelve month left if I'm lucky... lung cancer."

I felt genuinely sorry for him. He had turned his life around and now he was going to die.

"Do you think you can pot the fucker before I kick the bucket?"

"I promise," I said, with more conviction than I had a right to.

"Then, of course I'll give evidence."

John copped a statement there and then on one of the benches whilst I strolled around the grounds. I returned to John and Cole half an hour later and I wished Cole all the very best and I admit I had my fingers crossed that he would last until we got Coulter through the court.

My regret for Cole's unfortunate position was tempered by a growing sense of joy and satisfaction. I knew there was enough evidence now to prove that Coulter was a bad bastard. He had to be brought to book. I admit that I was over the moon.

I checked my phone as we were about to leave and noticed a missed call from Cliff Ambrose of the Drug Squad.

I had a lot to think about and couldn't face talking to him then. I'd call him when I got back to Bridgend.

18

The murder was still bothering me. Dai was keeping me updated, bringing me snippets of information but, to be honest, there wasn't a lot to go on. I seemed to spend most of my spare time checking through the information we had over and over again, looking for anything that might give us a lead when, Cliff from the Drug Squad, gave me another bell. This time I answered. He asked how it was all going. I had forgotten about his call to me when I was talking to Lloyd Cole and I kicked myself for not returning it. I apologised for not calling him back and brought him up to speed with the case, in the hope he might reciprocate with some nugget of information that might kick-start things again, but he didn't seem all that concerned. I hid my disappointment. He had only rung me to arrange a drink. We agreed to meet one night for a sherbet or two. I replaced the handset just as Dai burst into the office. He was like an excited Labrador puppy that had just seen his favourite toy.

"I may have a lead," he said.

"Dai, cool down now," I smiled. "You'll have a sodding heart attack. What have you got?"

"I think I've found out who he is."

I jumped up from my seat. "Who is he, Dai?"

"I think he's from the Rhondda and used to live in a caravan on Trecco. A bloke called Billy Hughes. He fits the bill, but it's all second-hand..."

"What do you mean, second hand?"

Dai's excited expression began to lose its attraction.

"Well, I was over Trecco last night and I met a young lady. We got talking and I just happened to mention the body in the dunes. She said, 'Have you spoken to my dad? He used to be on security at the camp, he knew everyone.' So, I rang the bloke direct, he's in Spain at the moment, back later today. He dropped the name Billy Hughes. I've been through the databases and there is a Billy Hughes, but his last bit of form is more than ten years ago. He hasn't been reported missing though."

"Okay," I said. "What time are you meeting this bloke?"

"Six o'clock, in the Dirty Duck."

"Dai, I hope you're right."

John stayed with us to write up the latest developments in the growing file of evidence against Coulter and that released me to spend a bit more time with Dai. I was feeling good. Things were beginning to slot into place.

19

The days of the Dirty Duck were numbered. It was a pub renowned throughout South Wales and was usually busy, especially on weekends; well, you'd expect it to be with three-and-a-half-thousand caravans on site and most of those able to house up to six holidaymakers. The problem for the Dirty Duck was the new owners of Trecco Bay. They had their own plans for the site and had built an entertainment complex complete with nightclub and bar. The Dirty Duck was offering beer at a lower price than the complex, but that wouldn't be enough to save it. The licensee was biding his time, making the most of the trade that had begun to dwindle day by day. He gave us a nod and, before our arses hit the lounge chairs, a couple of pints appeared in front of us. We hadn't been in there five minutes when a tall, athletic bloke with a thick black moustache, and obviously recently benefitting from a bit of Benidorm sun, entered and sat down next to us. He reminded me of Tom Selleck off that *Magnum P.I.* series. I looked out the window, just in case he had left his red Ferrari outside. Then I remembered the Dirty Duck was in a pedestrian-only area.

"Which one of you did I speak to last night?" Magnum asked.

"Me," said Dai.

"Look, I don't really want to get involved, but this is

all I know," Magnum looked around furtively before continuing. "Billy just left the site one day, no warning or anything. I knew him because I had to warn him off a few times. He was selling dope on the site. Funny thing is the caravan he used to live in was torched around about the same time as he left. I haven't seen 'im since. I finished here a couple of years ago."

"Do you know where he's from, family, anything?" Dai said.

Magnum shook his head. "No, just somewhere up the Rhondda."

"Will you make a statement?" Dai asked.

"Fuck no. I don't want to get involved."

There was no point pushing him. Few people ever wanted to help when drugs and murder were involved. I slipped him a twenty and, with my tongue firmly in my cheek, I thanked him for his 'public spirit.'

As we moved to go, he said, "I think he was narking to the Drug Squad, they were always around. I know they weren't happy with him 'cos he told me he was shitting 'imself. I'm sure it was your lot that torched his van."

I looked at Dai and we said nothing, just left in silence.

As we sat in the car, I knew Dai and I were on the same page. "Dai, I hope this is not what I think it might be..."

Dai looked at me and just raised his eyebrows.

83

20

We got back to my office and I opened the bottom drawer of my desk. "Dai, I need a drink, butt. I don't like where this is taking us."

I noticed Dai smiling at the piles of files littering the floor of my office. "Don't bloody grin at them. I'll get you to sort them out if you're not careful," I joked.

He held up his hands. "No, it's okay, boss. Nice to see you have your flaws too."

"Flaws? I don't have any flaws, what the hell are you talking about?" I said, unable to keep a straight face.

My nice bottle of malt was half full, or was it half empty? With the new turn of events, it was looking pretty empty to me. I poured us each a large shot in a pair of glasses that were well overdue for a wash. We both sat in silence for a few minutes. Was my corruption enquiry now about to extend beyond Coulter? Could our colleagues in the Drug Squad be involved in this murder? It was bad enough having Coulter to deal with.

"How should we play it, boss, all guns blazing, or on the Q.T?"

I held up my empty hand. "Hang on now, Dai. Let's think it through. Is Billy our victim? If he is, why kill him like they did? Is it gang related? I have to be honest, I have absolutely no idea. Have you got his last known address?"

Dai took a gulp of my malt. "Yes. There was a Billy

Hughes registered at an address in Porth, up the Rhondda, on the last census."

I was thinking hard. I could feel my head throb with the effort. "Okay, we'll get up there in the morning and crack on, but we'll have to be very discreet. Only you and I know about the Drug Squad involvement with him. Let's keep it that way."

"What about the Coulter case? How's that going?"

"It'll have to sit in my drawer for a while."

"Coincidence?"

I shrugged my shoulders. "Who knows? I'd like to think there was nothing in either case, but it's looking pretty stinky at the minute."

Dai left me alone to my tortured thoughts and I stared at the mess of files. I had always hated the paperwork side of the job but I knew I'd have to sort the mess out soon. I could always get DC Roger Bailey in if he stepped out of line and chuckled to myself at the thought of the poor bugger up to his neck in brown folders.

* * *

The following morning, Dai and I made our way to Porth. We drove up the valley, a desolate shit-hole of a place; shops now boarded up, but a place once the pride of Wales. Everything was as grey as the rain clouds seemingly stalking us above. It was like a scene from that book by Edgar Rice Burroughs, *The Land that Time Forgot*, but with a different kind of dinosaur stalking the valley. We pulled up outside a nicely painted terraced house. It stood out against the neighbouring grim, grey versions either side of it. The front garden was paved at some time in the past and the odd weed had started to show through the cracks in the slabs.

Dai checked the slate number affixed to the wall next to the front door. "This is it, number 9."

I knocked the door and a pretty woman, aged about thirty-five, with short, bobbed, blonde hair, greeted us. I could see her do a double take at Dai, another fair maiden smitten instantly by his lucky genes. She smiled at him and then frowned at me as I identified us. She invited us in for coffee. I wondered if she would have been as amenable if I hadn't had Errol Flynn with me?

The inside of the house was clean and tidy and smelt like lavender. I spotted one of those plug-in odour dispensers in the hallway and wondered if they would work in a smelly CID office. We followed her into a small living room dominated by an enormous flat screen television. She gestured towards the settee, and Dai and I sat whilst she went off the make the coffee.

"Attractive woman," Dai said casually.

"Keep your mind on the job, Dai."

He looked offended. "Just saying, boss."

We watched a snippet of a rom-com that was being broadcast on the big screen and I thought Dai was enjoying it a little too much.

Mrs Hughes returned with the coffees and pulled a footstool from an armchair and shuffled it close to Dai where she sat and smiled at him.

"What do you think of the coffee?" she asked Dai. He took a sip and smiled. "It's lovely. The best I've tasted."

I shook my head. "Bloody hell," I muttered under my breath. Then at normal volume I said, "Yes, it's lovely," but Mrs Hughes didn't seem interested in my opinion. If I wasn't happily married, I'd have felt hurt.

"Mrs Hughes? We're making enquiries regarding Billy Hughes. Do you know him?" I asked her.

She forced her gaze from Dai for a second to answer me. "Yes, you could say that," she said. "What's he been up to now?"

"I just need to know whatever you can tell me about him?"

She sighed. She didn't seem happy to be speaking about him. "I was married to him for a few years, but haven't seen him for about seven. He doesn't live here and I want nothing to do with him. He left me in the lurch with a young baby to bring up alone. As far as I'm concerned, he's dead. The last I heard, he was working on the fairground in Porthcawl."

"Well, Mrs Hughes, we believe he *is* dead," I said. I didn't want to mess about. I needed to get this tied up neatly, but perhaps I could have been a bit more delicate. Thankfully, it didn't seem to come as a shock to her. She just looked at me without any expression I could read and said, "Would you like that coffee or a cup of tea?"

After about an hour and having obtained all the

antecedent history we could, Dai took a statement from her. She seemed to be quite pleased that Dai was sitting next to her as he wrote the statement.

"Is there anyone who would be able to formally identify him, apart from you, Mrs Hughes?" Dai asked.

"His mam and dad have passed away over ten years ago... I suppose I'm the only one the bastard had."

"Okay," Dai said. "I'll make the necessary arrangements, perhaps tomorrow about ten? I'll fix up the transport for you. Is that okay?"

"Yes, that's no problem."

Dai then drove me slowly back down the valley until we reached civilisation and a break in the grey clouds.

21

I tasked DC Roger Bailey with the job of collecting Mrs Hughes and conveying her to the mortuary at the hospital. I guessed that would upset Mrs Hughes more than viewing the body of her former husband. Even someone as inexperienced as me could sense an attraction towards our Dai and it was something I wasn't wanting to encourage with a thirty-minute car journey together. I didn't have to ask Dai if he felt the same towards the woman because I knew Dai was attracted to anything that moved, as long as it was female.

Me and Dai were already at the mortuary, watching a white-clad porter getting the body prepared for a viewing. In fairness, the resident technicians hadn't done a bad job on Billy, considering what the poor bloke had been through, even his face looked half decent, although a little bit contorted. You would never have guessed he'd met such a violent death and been on ice for five years.

Mrs Hughes arrived on time and, in fairness, was quite calm and relaxed and smiled warmly when she saw Dai. I accompanied her into the viewing room and asked the million-dollar question, "Is that your husband, Billy Hughes?"

She stared at him for a few seconds, turned, looked at me with a tear in her eye and said, "Yes, that's him... he wasn't always a twat, you know?" she whispered. "He had some good points, but I'm buggered if can remember what they were now."

"Did Billy have any tattoos?"

She nodded. "Usual chav stuff," she said. "He had 'Love' and 'Hate' on his knuckles."

I pulled his arms out from under the sheet. "Are these the tattoos?"

"Yes. I did them for him with a needle and blue ink many years ago. We were just kids."

"Nice!" What else could I say? Couldn't really say they looked like shit, could I?

"Thank you, Mrs Hughes."

I told DC Bailey to take a statement of identification and convey the lady home. All in all, not a bad day's work and I was feeling optimistic, but that wasn't going to last long. The shit storm was soon to follow.

22

I was just about to leave the office to have an early night, as I knew the next few days were going to be a roller coaster and I wanted to get some well overdue rest when the phone rang. I was in two minds about leaving it ringing. It was my old mate, Cliff Ambrose, from the Drug Squad.

"You on for that drink?"

"Sure. Time and place?"

"No time like the present," he suggested. "See you at seven in the Castle."

I hung up and then thought about Cliff's timing. I had only seen him two or three times in twenty-odd years and now he was ringing me for a drink? Was Cliff involved in all this shit? No, he couldn't be, surely? Anyway, I cleared my head with a coffee, made my way to the charge room and cadged a lift into town with one of the uniform lads.

Cliff was the typical Drug Squad officer. He always had the long hair, stubble, he dressed the part of a down and out and loved being in the company of the vermin who peddled shit to the kids on the street. I often wondered if he too was a user. He was so full of crap, a cocky, arrogant man with a self-belief in his own intelligence that went way beyond the reality, but he got results. He was very well thought of and a brilliant undercover officer. On promotion, he had headed up the Force Drug Squad, and they were certainly still producing the goods.

I ordered a pint and sat in the corner of the snug. The open fire was a welcome I appreciated, and the place had a lovely warm atmosphere, low oak beams as black and shiny as coal with horse brass ornaments tacked along the length of each. The bar was small with sparkling clean mirrors behind that cast the bright light from the down lighters out into the otherwise dimly lit seating area.

When Ambrose walked in, I was surprised that he hadn't altered since the last time I had seen him. He still had the swagger, still full of confidence and still looking like the vermin he dealt with. I let him get his own pint; he earned more than me, and he sat opposite on a stool. For the next hour, we chewed the fat, laughed at past indiscretions and talked about friends who had passed, and we both wondered how we actually managed to stay in the job. Then, like a bolt out of the blue, it came.

"Any progress with the 'ice-man cometh' case, Ter?"

I was instantly on guard. I wondered if this was just professional interest. But I smelt a rat.

"No, no further on, Cliff," I said. "Winding it right down, no leads, nothing, just dead ends."

"File it, Terry, *put it on ice*," he laughed at his own joke, and even added "Lol."

Twat!

"Move on, butt," he added sagely.

I thought about what he was saying and nodded my head. We sank a few more pints and later went our separate ways, promising we'd not leave it so long until the next time. I stepped outside and called the station and got through to DC Bailey. He said he'd pick me up and drop me home so I popped back into the pub for a small Irish whilst I waited. I had a terrible gut feeling that my old mate Cliff was up to his neck in this pile of shit. But how would I prove it, and did I really want to add another copper to my file marked 'Bent Bastards'?

I got home around one-thirty in the morning and Molly was fast asleep. It took her over ten years to get used to my being absent most nights and she suffered from exhaustion and no doubt depression for a while. Being a copper's wife was not easy. Being the wife of a detective was even worse. Many marriages ended in divorce. It took a special kind of woman to stick it out with a detective. My Molly was one of those special women. She knew I wasn't like Dai. I was never in the same league as him when it came to women. I'm a smidge over six foot tall and still at my fighting weight of twelve-and-a-half stone. I don't keep myself fit but I guess I've been blessed with a fast metabolism. I would never call myself good looking but I don't think I'm ugly either. Molly says I look strong, rugged and well lived-in. I think that was a compliment. She certainly seemed to be happy with my appearance. I've still got most of my hair, though it's beginning to wave me goodbye. I had recently shaved off the moustache that I'd had since I first met Molly, and she wasn't happy I'd removed it, so it was beginning to make a comeback with the addition of a goatee. The goatee was still on probation. The pay of a DI wasn't bad, but we never seemed to have two pennies to rub together. It seemed that every time we had some cash, something would come along and take it off us. Car repairs, broken appliances, and just about anything that *could* go wrong *would* go wrong and we'd end up worse off than before. How the hell did that work? We didn't have much, but at least we were happy. If I was honest, I sometimes suspected that Molly was so used to me being away that she'd possibly become more comfortable on her own.

I cracked open a can of beer and sat in front of the telly and set it to subtitles so I could watch something in silence and not disturb my Molly. It was the usual old load of shite. I remembered there being only three or four channels. Now we had over a hundred and they were all a waste of time and money. Absolute bollocks. I flicked through a few of the options then switched it off.

I sat quietly in the dark, can in hand, and tried to think about anything other than the 'Frozen' case. As was usual, I failed miserably. Images of poor Billy lying in the dunes, plastic wrapped and having spent five years in a freezer like a bag of frozen peas, kept flashing through my mind. Links to the Drug Squad were to be expected where druggies were concerned. It was a bit like pasties being linked to bakers or dogs being linked to vets. But something about Cliff bothered me. Intuition? Perhaps twenty-odd years of dealing with scum developed a sixth sense? Whatever it was, it wouldn't be ignored.

23

Although slightly hung over, I was back at my desk by 7am.

What should I do? What was the way forward?

Before I got a chance to think it through, the young policewoman knocked on my door and entered my office. I looked up and dreaded what was coming. I admit that had it been a young male copper I'd have told him to sling his hook, but this young woman reminded me of my Molly when she was the same age. "WPC…?"

"Williams, sir."

"Any relation to DS Williams?"

She shook her head. "Not that I'm aware of, sir."

"That's a shame," I said.

She looked puzzled and I didn't tell her that it was a shame she wasn't related because if she were it would be unlikely that Dai would try to get inside her knickers. Mind you, knowing Dai…

"What can I do for you, you still dealing with 'The Dick of the Dunes?'"

"Yes, sir. The sergeant dropped it in my lap. Said it would be good for my career if I could catch him."

"And?"

She looked sheepish. "Well, sir. I was wondering if you'd consider letting me do an aide with CID?"

"An aide?"

"Yes, sir. I've got three years' service and I'm pretty

good at my job. I've nicked more bodies than most of the guys on my shift and I'm certainly not a dumb blonde."

"I can see that."

"The way I see it, sir, is if you take me on as an aide, I can help you with the murder and work on the 'Prick from the Park' job..."

"Dick of the Dunes," I corrected her.

"Yes, sir."

"If I take you on, you'll have to get to know the difference between a Dick and a Prick. I don't want Dai or any of the others trying to show you."

She laughed. She had a sense of humour, a definite prerequisite to be a detective.

"Do what you can on the Dick of the Dunes and I'll see what I can do."

She grinned. "Thank you, sir. I won't let you down."

I held up my hand. "Can't promise anything, but I'll have a word and see what I can do."

She stood to attention and I shook my head. "You can forget all that official bollocks if you're going to be part of my team."

"Yes, sir."

"And you can stop calling me sir, makes me feel old. The others call me boss."

She nodded and turned on her heel to leave me alone to think about my next move.

My first priority was to let my DCI know about the case and what my suspicions were. He'd be the third person to know, and in my mind, that was two too many but protocol demanded it. I gave him a bell and arranged to meet him at HQ, solely because I knew I'd have to go through him before the case was blown open. The ACC Crime might not like it but I had to keep to the chain of command.

My DCI, Ron Evans, was old school. He had over thirty years in the job and had been a detective for most of his service. He was as wide as he was tall and had recently shaved off the white comb-over that had made him the focus of much ridicule – behind his back. He looked better. His face was always red and bore the scars of a lifetime of alcohol excess. His bulbous nose shone like Rudolph the reindeer and he looked like his liver wouldn't stand much more of the abuse he had subjected it to. I didn't think he was an alcoholic. He had never turned up for work drunk – unlike some officers I'd known over the years – but he was definitely too partial to a drink to expect him to live a long and healthy retirement. I also felt sorry for him. He had been one of life's unlucky characters. His only child had died in a motorcycle accident ten years ago and his wife had died shortly after from what he had always claimed was a broken heart. He had no one and I understood his reluctance to retire. Ron played everything with a straight bat and talked even straighter. I brought him up to speed on the Billy Hughes enquiry.

His reaction? "Fuck me, Terry. Do you realise what you're alleging? A senior officer involved in corruption going back years and another possibly involved with a murder? You better be fucking spot on, or we're both for the chop."

"Chief, I'm not a hundred per cent sure, but it's certainly looking that way," I said. "How do you want us to take it forward from here?" I said, even though I knew he would ultimately have no say in it. I would take my lead from the ACC but it paid to be tactful with the chain of command.

"Look, you go and prepare a press release on the murder, make it national. I'm going upstairs to speak to the Super. Fuck, this will get their juices flowing. Leave it to me, I'll speak to you later."

I got hold of the Force Press Liaison Officer and scripted the release, the usual pro-forma type of shit.... *'Anybody with any info, please contact, blaa, blaa, blaa-de blaa.'*

24

Later in the day, after the release had gone national, I called Dai to my office, same old routine, a glass of malt and we discussed progress, or lack of it.

"Anything from the press release, Dai?"

"Nothing much, boss. The usual crank calls, nothing that will take us any further forward." Dai looked worried. "What's your take on it?"

"My take, Dai? I'm confused. Cliff might be smelly and somehow know more about this murder than he is letting on, but why would the killer keep the body frozen?"

"Could Ambrose be the killer?"

I shook my head. "I doubt it. He's holding back on us but he has too much to lose."

"Perhaps Billy was going to dob Ambrose and his team to Professional Standards?"

I shrugged. The truth was we just didn't have a clue and were fishing for something, however small, something that would give us a break. "Surely keeping a body on ice is a stupid thing to do, especially for someone in Ambrose's position? If he was involved, he could have got rid of it before now."

Dai snorted. "You know what he's like, he's an arrogant bastard. Who knows what he was thinking? He probably didn't think anyone would have the nerve to take him on. That's if he really *is* involved?"

"Let me tell you, Dai, I'm pretty sure he's involved

somehow, make no bones about it. Why else is he suddenly so interested in the case and keen for me to drop it? I don't want to believe it but we owe it to Billy. That's no way for a bloke to die even if he was a scumbag drug supplier. No, there's more to this and I'm afraid if Cliff is involved, others are probably up to their necks in shit too. Let's crack on in the morning with Cliff's time line, perhaps we can tie it down?"

I just put the malt away and the phone rang. "Boss? There's a woman on the phone from Ireland, says she has info on the Billy Hughes case."

"Put her through," I told the metallic voice on the switchboard. I waited for the connection. "DI Terry McGuire. Who's speaking?"

A worried sounding woman identified herself as Anne Evans. "I'm ex job," she said, "but had to quit in 2011 after having a bit of a meltdown," she continued. "I'd been part of Cliff's elite squad back in the day. I saw the press release on Facebook and knew Billy. I could write a book about him."

I stopped her. I didn't want her to go any further on the phone, so she gave me her contact number and I rang her straight back to confirm. She told me she was now living in Ireland so I made arrangements to meet her in the Ashling Hotel in Dublin at 2 pm the next day.

I hung up the phone and spoke to Dai. "This could be it, butt. Do some background with Personnel Records on Anne Evans. First thing in the morning, I'll take an early flight to Dublin. Keep me updated."

A trip to Dublin. It felt like my birthday.

25

I got a call from Ron later. He told me the ACC had given the go ahead for a full background check on Cliff and I had full access to his and any other records, going way back to when we joined together. I only hoped that I'd find something in the file that would point me in the right direction.

The time period I was particularly interested in was from the 1st of January 2011 to the present. I must say, Cliff had a pretty impressive record, no wonder he flew up the ranks. He'd received commendations for this, commendations for that, secondments here, secondments there. Undercover work all over the country, this bloke was a one-man crime-busting machine, but still an arrogant twat.

I then picked up on a date in 2010. Cliff was a DS and, together with four DCs, he was used for covert surveillance throughout South Wales. Their remit was to gather intelligence on major drug suppliers, by any means necessary. Money for informants was no object. I also discovered that one of the targets was a little shit called Elwyn Fowler from Porthcawl. Elwyn's name had cropped up more than once now in the investigation. He was a top drug supplier, a mean, sly son of a bitch. However, he got killed in a road accident a couple of years back. A few other things cropped up that could seem insignificant but what the hell? Cliff had divorced about ten years ago and now lived alone in a large isolated Victorian house on the outskirts of Bridgend. The squad was disbanded mid 2011, again due to budget and financial restraints. Cliff got promoted to DI and was then seconded to Scotland Yard for the next four years. Cliff continued to build a reputation up in the smoke, second to none as the European Drugs Coordinator, travelling all over Europe, liaising with all major police forces. When he returned to South Wales, he was promoted to his present position.

I closed the file and sat back, thinking that Cliff looked like he'd become an even bigger twat. All I needed now was that one break so I could really go to town on the bastard.

I usually gave my wife a call each day, especially if I was on a prolonged enquiry. It couldn't be easy being at home and wondering what I was up to. I was about to call Molly to check on her when I suddenly realised there was someone else I could talk to for some background on Cliff – his ex-wife. From what I'd heard so far, I didn't think there'd be much loyalty left between them. It was worth a try. I called the Personnel Department at HQ and spoke to one of the civilian clerks.

"Hi, this is Terry McGuire, Bridgend DI. Is there any way you can give me some ancient history on one of our own, please?"

The voice was cautious and clearly reluctant to get involved. "I'm sorry, sir. Don't think I'm able to do that. Data Protection rules and..."

I stopped her mid-sentence. "I understand there are certain procedures, etcetera, but this is important to a case we're working on. It's a murder and I believe the information could be vital to cracking it open." It didn't seem to make much difference but I managed to get her to pass me over to the admin manager who was far more forthcoming.

I related the details of the DCI and I could hear a sharp intake of breath on the other end of the line. "You sure about this?" the manager asked.

"I'm very sure," I replied. "I promise to keep you out of this if it goes tits-up."

"I don't need to look up the contact," the manager explained. "Cliff Ambrose's wife was bridesmaid at my wedding. She's still a good friend of mine and I can assure you she'll be pretty happy to help you. She hates his guts."

I made a note of the name and address and tucked the note into my jacket pocket. I called Dai in from the office, told him what I was going to do and asked him to get WPC Williams from uniform downstairs to speak to me. Within five minutes the young copper was standing at my office door.

"Get your civvies on," I said. "I need you to come with me for an interview."

She grinned and disappeared. She returned in record time, dressed in jeans and a T-shirt and a denim jacket.

We took the pool car and I let her drive.

I realised that I only knew her surname. I liked to be on first name terms with my detectives and whilst she wasn't one yet, if she proved herself to me she'd certainly get an aide on the department. "What's your name?"

"Caroline," she said.

I noticed she was controlling the car in the classic driving school manner, hands at ten-to-two and she was nice and smooth through the gearbox. "When did you do the driving course?"

"About eighteen months ago," she said. "Something wrong?"

"No, nothing," I grinned.

Caroline was an attractive young woman and I was always intrigued at what made a woman want to become a copper. I usually got the same old crap, 'I want to help society...' blah, blah, bloody blah, but Caroline continued to surprise me. "I drifted into it. I had no idea what I wanted to do. I'd worked in a shop and found it boring and then I heard there was an intake coming up and I fancied wearing the uniform and having my own truncheon to keep me entertained on quiet nights," she said.

I almost missed it, but I saw her grin as she checked the rear-view mirror and I began to laugh.

She certainly had the humour to make a detective. I was warming to her.

We arrived at the home of Ambrose's wife. It was an insignificant semi in a small new-build estate on the outskirts of Cardiff.

Juliette Johnson was waiting at the door; she looked eager to speak to us. She explained that she remarried a couple of years after Cliff dumped her.

We entered and sat in the cosy lounge at the front of the house. An elderly lady was hovering in the kitchen and Juliette called her for teas all round.

"That's Cliff's mum," she whispered.

I was shocked.

"She came to live with me after Cliff left. They don't get on. He's always been a bit of a bastard to her. I know it's strange, but she prefers to be with me and David."

"David?" Caroline asked. I was happy to let Caroline take the lead.

"My husband. He's a complete contrast to Cliff."

"In what way?" Caroline asked again.

"David is loving. He cares about people. How many blokes do you know who would be prepared to let the ex-mother-in-law of your new wife live with you?"

"Good point," agreed Caroline.

"David is a nurse in the Heath Hospital. He's at work just now, but I rang him to tell him you were coming."

"And is he okay with us being here?" I asked.

"He'd rather we just forget about Cliff, especially after the last time..."

"The last time?"

Juliette nodded. "It was about a year after Cliff threw me out of our home. I met David and he was staying the night with me. I was staying with Cliff's mother. She was good to me and had no problem with me seeing someone else. Cliff turns up at the door, pretending he wanted to see his mother. Someone must have told him I was seeing someone else and he couldn't have liked it."

I was confused. "I thought he left you?"

"He did, but he's a control freak. Guess he hadn't planned for me to find happiness so quickly. He didn't like it."

Caroline leaned forward, totally engrossed. "What did he do?"

"He forced his way in and dragged David from bed. He tried to give him a kicking but he didn't know David's a third Dan black belt. Cliff came off worse. He really didn't like that. Next thing we know, there are parking tickets littering our screen wherever we go, we get flat tyres and even a cut brake pipe."

Caroline was shocked. "Jesus!"

"Nothing you could prove, I suppose?" I said.

She shook her head. "Too clever for that. He's a vindictive bastard. I'll never know what I saw in him."

"What *did you* see in him?" I said.

She thought for a moment. "I guess it was the excitement. You know, he was an undercover copper, dealing with crime, keeping the streets safe from the dealers. At least that's what I thought."

This was sounding promising. "What do you mean?"

"You've got to understand Cliff. He's very...

complicated. Always wanted to be the best at everything he does. He was brought up in a rough estate in the Rhondda and would do anything he could to get out of there."

"That's not such as bad thing," Caroline observed, and I wondered if there was some parallel with her own backstory? Wouldn't be unusual for a copper. My backstory was pretty much the same.

Juliette shrugged. "You need to speak to his mother. She could tell you things that would make your teeth curl. I wish she'd told me before we married."

I was really into this now. "What sort of things?"

The old lady entered and I shut up. She placed the pot of tea on the coffee table between us and smiled. I got the impression that not all was functioning properly behind her eyes.

I waited for the old lady to close the door behind her and tried again. "What sort of things?"

Juliette handed out the tea and sighed. "When Cliff was ten or eleven, he'd set fire to the grass verges around the estate because his dad was a part-time fireman who got paid on call-outs."

"Enterprising." Caroline grinned.

"Until one of his fires spread to the estate and two houses burnt to the ground. He was lucky nobody was hurt. His dad covered Cliff's tracks for him and no one was the wiser."

"Anything else?"

"He started smoking pot when he was thirteen. He

never broke the habit either. He'd often bring pot or cocaine home with him. He'd sit in the kitchen and get off his face. Then he'd expect me to be... friendly. I told him I didn't want that shit in the house. I was terrified he'd get caught. We had a decent house and decent pay and I could see him losing everything. But then he started getting promoted and I just let it go. I thought he must be doing something right to keep rising through the ranks."

I shook my head.

"Then he got to Detective Chief Inspector and moved me out. He closed our accounts and I was left with nowhere to go and no money. As I said, Cliff's mother let me stay with her for a while and then I got this place and she sold up and moved in with Ame. No sooner had we split than he started spending money like it was water. He'd turn up and give his mother a fistful of twenties. She never wanted his money, she wanted his time and love, but that was something Cliff could never give. Oh, he pretended he could, but I soon got to realise that it was all an act. Then his mother told me she believed he was a psychopath."

Caroline was shocked. "A what?"

I held up my hand. "It's not unusual for people in top jobs being labelled as psychopaths. Something about the need to be in control?"

Juliette clearly agreed. "I did a bit of research on it. Cliff has all the signs."

I drank some of my tea. It was some herbal

nonsense but at least it was hot and wet. "Anything specific you can tell us, dates, events that you can pin down?"

Juliette placed her cup on her saucer and back onto the tray.

"I remember him telling me something about a druggie in Porthcawl. It was just before he was promoted to Chief. He came home one night and said something about this guy needing to be put in his place."

"Could this be Billy, the guy we found in the dunes?"

"I can't swear by it but I know he was really wound up for a while and then he was happy again overnight. I can't pin it down but it would have been about five years ago, no doubt about that."

We talked some more for a little while before Caroline and I left.

"No statement, sir?" she said to me as we walked to the car.

"No point," I explained. "She can't be specific and it would only draw her back into a dodgy situation with Cliff. Best left alone."

Caroline was quiet for a moment, concentrating on her driving. Then she nudged me with her elbow. "So, at what rank do these psychopathic tendencies kick in... sir?" She chuckled.

It wasn't lost on me.

"Must be Chief Inspector," I grinned.

I got Caroline to drop me at home and Molly was

standing in the window. She didn't look too pleased to see an attractive woman dropping me home.

I had a trip to Ireland in the morning and I could do without any friction from Molly. Thankfully, she was okay and she packed my holdall for a possible overnight. Mind you, she did ask if I was travelling alone. Bless her!

26

I arrived at Dublin airport and I made my way to the Ashling Hotel by taxi.

On the way, my phone was knocking up the charges as Dai was filling me in on Anne's antecedents. "By all accounts a good, honest, hard-working officer, who eventually ended up on the Drug Squad," he said. "However, she left the job due to stress, had a bit of a breakdown."

The taxi dropped me off outside the front door to the hotel. It was a decent looking place. Close to the Heuston rail station and the zoo, I guessed it was probably popular with visitors to the fair city. From the outside, it looked like it was built in the seventies. The ground floor external walls were clad in large, dark granite tiles and the windows in the upper floors were set in an expensive, light-coloured large-scale tile. The glass doors opened and a concierge stepped out to greet me. "Good day to ya, sir."

I always took an overnight bag, just in case I had to stay longer than I intended to, and I lugged my holdall out of the trunk and kept it away from the eager tip-seeker. "I can manage," I said.

The smartly dressed man smiled. "From Wales?"

"Bridgend."

"Are you staying with us, Mr...?"

"McGuire, Terry McGuire."

"McGuire? Good Irish name, may I add?"

I had to hand it to him; he knew how to chat a tip out of a stone. "My dad was from Roscommon," I admitted. I wasn't going to divulge my occupation. Although Ireland is a magical place, coppers from the UK still tended to keep their job a secret out there. It was a hangover from the days of the Troubles in the North. British coppers represented the hated British establishment and it was best not to take a chance by announcing I was an inspector, too.

"Just meeting someone," I explained.

The man stepped aside. "Welcome to the Ashling Hotel, sir."

I walked through the door with a brass sign declaring it as the 'Iveagh Bar' of the hotel, a warm and welcoming place. I could image sitting next to the bar and the recessed fire and drinking copious amounts of Guinness and Bushmills. There was a family sitting in a large, comfortable looking settee, and my eyes were drawn to a petite brunette, sitting alone in a corner, facing the entrance door. She smiled and I knew immediately that it was Anne. She rose to meet me and her tiny hand was lost in my meaty mitt. I detected a slight tremble, she seemed understandably nervous. I introduced myself. "Do you want a drink?"

"No, thank you, I already have one."

I sat down beside her and beckoned the waiter. Since I was in Ireland, I decided I'd indulge, "A double Bushmills, please."

The waiter nodded, smiled and left us alone. We chatted about the weather and Dublin and the friendly Irish people; then my drink arrived and I had to cut to the chase. "Anne, you obviously know about the enquiry. What can you tell me?"

She nodded. "Well, I first met Billy when I joined the surveillance team run by Cliff Ambrose. Billy was one of his narks, they went back years. Most of Billy's info was on Elwyn Fowler. He used to get well paid for it, too. Billy lived in a caravan just up from Rhych Point on Trecco Bay, but we'd normally meet him over the dunes by the gravels."

Another piece in the jigsaw? That couldn't be a coincidence.

"You mean the gravel pits?"

"Yes, over in Newton. I really enjoyed the work, but one day Cliff approached me in the locker room and handed me an envelope. 'This is for you,' he said. I opened it and it was stuffed full of tenners. 'There's two hundred there, Anne. That's your share,' he said to me. I was flabbergasted, 'what's it for?' I asked. 'It's from Billy, his last info was worth two grand, that's a grand for Billy and two hundred each for us,' he told me. I thrust the envelope back in his hand and just ran out of the locker room. I was crying and felt sick to my stomach. I didn't know what to do. I went straight home. I couldn't sleep, believing my partners were corrupt. I rang in sick the following day and stayed off for a fortnight; I couldn't face them."

Her hand shook a little more as she took a sip of her drink. "I believed that incident started my depression and breakdown. I had no one to turn to in the squad; they were a law unto themselves."

"A few days later, I related the incident to a DS I knew I could trust. He advised me to report it, but how could I, who would they believe? So I never did. I only went back for another week, but the rest of them gave me the cold shoulder. I came off the squad then, in fact I never worked again. It broke my heart and my mind. I went on long-term sick and finished six months later. I only had ten years in."

I felt sorry for her. I knew coppers could close ranks and make things awkward for others not singing from the same hymn sheet. "When was this, Anne, and who were the other three detectives?"

"It was early January 2011. The three were DCs Ken Stevens, Alan Green and Peter James. I would think they've all finished now."

"Do you know what happened to Billy?"

"No, I don't, I swear. I only know that his van was torched when I was off for that fortnight."

"Do you think Cliff and the others are involved in Billy's murder, Anne?"

"I honestly wouldn't put it past them. They're all bent as butcher's hooks."

"Would you make a statement, accounting for all of this?"

"Of course. Perhaps it will give me some closure? I

feel relieved now that I've spoken to you, Terry. Thank you for listening to me. I didn't think anyone ever would."

"No, thank you. Now where's that waiter? I need two doubles after that."

I used the job-financed taxi to take Anne home. She lived just outside Dublin. Ballintearly Farm was a smallholding where she lived with her sister and brother-in-law. Life, post-job, seemed good for her and I believed it would get even better.

I took a full detailed statement from her, kissed her on the cheek and thanked her.

I flew straight back to Cardiff airport. I was literally as high as a kite. I knew I had them all now, the corrupt murdering bastards.

27

I had already rung my boss, Ron, and brought him up to speed with the information that Anne had supplied. He, in turn, had arranged an urgent conference with the ACC Crime and the Crown Prosecution Service in the ACC's office in Headquarters.

I attended at the appointed time and laid out all the relevant evidence and information. Dai had come with me for support, not that I needed support but, as things were about to get complicated, I wanted Dai up to speed on everything to help me out. All seemed to be going well until the CPS solicitor, Reginald Archer, threw a big spanner in the works. That was nothing unusual with that lot of tossers from the CPS. Unless you give them everything on a platter, they wouldn't go after a pisser.

"Where's the evidence, Terry? All you have is an unstable ex-police officer who has suddenly come out of the woodwork. You have nothing concrete. Supposition and speculation, it doesn't convict. I'm sorry, I don't think we could even do them for corruption on her say-so."

I was tamping mad. "Oh, fuck you, then. I'll get the evidence, one way or another."

I gathered up all my papers and stormed out, closely followed by Dai. We got back to the nick and regrouped, Dai made the coffee whilst I began planning our next strategy.

The phone rang. It was Ron.

"That was a bit unprofessional, wasn't it, Terry? Anyway, I've smoothed it all over. You carry on; do what you've got to do to put these bastards away."

It was good to have the backing of the boss. I put the phone down as Dai walked in, handed me a coffee and slumped in the chair opposite my desk.

"What you reckon, Dai? Where do we go from here, butt?"

"You know Cliff better than anyone, boss. He's an arrogant son of a bitch, but maybe that could be his weakness?"

I was intrigued. "What do you mean, Dai?"

Dai stood and walked past me to the window behind my desk and stared through the grime-stained casement. "Well, he's shot up the ranks, his shit is chocolate. This bloke doesn't give a toss about anyone. Let's just say we feed him a few worms and see if he bites. I think he alone killed Billy and the three dickheads helped him dispose of the body and then torched the van."

It was worth a shot. "I'll give him a bell. I'll arrange a sherbet or two and see what develops. In the meantime, get the financials on them all... and their addresses. Could be we need to set up some surveillance after I've had a chat with him."

28

"Just like the old days, Terry? Two old mates talking about the old times, that's what it's all about. We haven't got long left in the job, so let's make the most of it. You got any plans, after retirement?"

"Not thought about it, to be honest, Cliff," I said honestly. I enjoyed the job too much to even think about finishing. I knew I'd have to think about it someday but I fully intended to complete my thirty and take anything else that was offered. "May stay on, and try and go up another notch. See how it goes?"

Cliff nodded as he sank half his pint. "I want to get my Super's Crown, do a year or two, then fuck off into the sunset."

"Sunset, you?"

"No, straight up. I've got a few properties, one in Portugal and one in Florida." He then gave me a big wink. *Arrogant twat.*

"Well I haven't really got a pot to piss in, truth be told, Cliff. But me and the missus are happy enough."

He snorted. "Best thing I did was get shot of the missus years ago. Paid her off, kept the house, everything is cushty, as Del Boy says." He finished his pint and held out his hand to get another round. "By the way, how's the Billy the Fish Finger case going? Lol." Yes, he actually spoke like he was on Facebook or something.

"Bit of progress," I said, as I watched his eyes. "Had a day in Ireland, couple of days ago..."

"Oh aye, bog snorkelling is it? Lol."

Arrogant bastard.

"No, following a lead." I finished my pint and slid the glass across the little round bar table. "Interviewed an ex-WDC, a woman called Anne Evans, one of your team. Never worked with her myself, but she knew Billy."

Well, I thought Cliff was going to choke. He started coughing and then found his composure. "That went down the wrong way," he said.

I bet it did. *Lol.*

"She was on your squad, so she told me."

"Aye," he admitted, with a dismissive wave of his hand. "I remember Anne. Bit neurotic. What did she have to say for herself?"

"Not a lot. Just that he was a nark for the squad, nothing more, bit of a waste of time."

"Oh aye, I remember Billy, small-time dealer, bottom feeder," Cliff stood to take the glasses to the bar. "How is Anne these days? Not a bad looker in her day. Went off her head, so they told me. Just didn't turn up for work one day. Did she mention me or the other boys?"

"No, to be honest, she didn't make a lot of sense, I didn't even bother to take a statement off her."

I could see Cliff was a bit concerned; I had obviously hit a nerve, and this reinforced my suspicions.

"Look, Ter, it's getting late. No point in getting another round of drinks. Fancy a nightcap at my place, see how the other half lives, eh?"

I was intrigued and agreed, so Cliff took the empties back to the bar and asked the barman to call us a taxi.

29

We travelled about two miles out of town, drove up a secluded country lane and came to a stop outside two ornate black metal gates. Cliff pressed his key fob and the gates opened slowly. I noticed CCTV cameras everywhere. The place was considerably upmarket compared to the one Cliff's ex-wife was living in. *Bastard!*

The taxi driver trundled up the wide pebbled drive, the gravel crunching under the tyres, and stopped outside the front door. Security lights came on as Cliff paid the driver. The house was spectacular.

"This is nice, butt."

"All bought and paid for, Terry. No mortgage on this. Five bedrooms, three bathrooms, games room, bar, the lot, butt," he grinned smugly.

I really didn't know this bloke. If he wasn't bent, I'd eat my hat.

"Stay the night, Terry? Crash out in the guest bedroom. You can have a good look around in the morning."

Aye, too royal I will.

We had several more shorts of some whisky Cliff swore cost him nearly fifty quid a bottle but was not a patch on my favourite, and then I crashed out.

A bright shaft of sun through the partially open curtains of the guest room woke me and I had a head like a bucket. I got my stuff together, swilled my face and spent a few minutes doing the necessary toiletries before I walked downstairs where Cliff was squeezing fresh orange juice.

"Coffee?" he asked.

"Aye, go on, my head's in the shed."

"Do you want a fry up?"

I groaned. "No thanks. A piece of toast will do." I sat on a kitchen stool beneath a white granite breakfast bar that must have cost the same as a small car.

"It's like Colditz here. Cameras, alarms, security lights..."

"Yes, Ter. Had to be done, butt. I was up the Yard five days a week, only made it home on the weekends, my safe-haven, I call it."

He popped two rounds of bread into a toaster that looked like something from the fifties but I guessed was a new and very expensive little number. "Look, I've got to pop into the office for a couple of hours," he said. "Will you be okay on your own until I come back? We can go for a spot of lunch." He set the timer on the toaster then turned with a smug grin. "I hope you've rung the missus and got your alibi all sorted?"

"Molly's fine. She's a good girl."

"My ex was a twat," he spat. "Never liked me working all hours. She liked me bringing home the bread and paying for fancy holidays and new cars but she always thought I was shagging around."

"And were you?"

He smiled. "If you've got it, flaunt it. That's what I say."

The toaster popped and the arrogant bastard left and gave me a free run of the house. I couldn't help myself. I had to have a nose around. I started opening drawers, 'skulking' I think it was called, not believing that he'd leave anything incriminating, he was too sharp for that.

I poked around in his bedroom and found a gold Rolex Oyster watch in his bedside cabinet. He also left an iPad on top of the bed but it was password protected.

I went outside and walked around the garden, it was then I noticed a relatively new build on the back of the house. No windows, a steel door with a double padlock.

He could not be that stupid, could he?

I checked for CCTV and could see two cameras on the rear wall. I went back inside the house and found the video controller in a cupboard under the stairs. I knew the tapes would probably be time-coded but I switched the unit off. I thought it was better that he found an interruption to his recordings and suspected something amiss than him actually seeing me messing about in his shed and other places that should be out of bounds to guests.

I looked for the keys to the shed but couldn't find them anywhere. I was intrigued. I returned to the back of the house and had another skulk, turning stones over, just in case he was too arrogant to be careful. To my amazement, I found keys under a large garden ornament. One of the keys fitted and I opened the padlock and pushed the heavy door. I stepped into the dark interior and put the light on. It was crammed full of stuff. There was a quad bike, a 650 Yamaha motorcycle, a pair of high-end grass strimmers, mowers and other gardening gear. Further in, I noticed a large green tarpaulin. I pulled it back to reveal two large chest freezers. I opened the first to find the usual – it was full of frozen stuff, legs of lamb, pork, beef and just about every other type of meat money can buy at a premium. I let the lid drop and opened the second. It was empty but still switched on. All it contained was empty freezer bags, and what appeared to be several long strands of blonde hair. I didn't know whether it was the chill from the freezer or the realisation that my old pal was possibly a killer that sent shivers up my spine? I slammed the lid, replaced the tarp, locked it all up and replaced the keys, just as I heard Cliff returning in his top-of-the-range Mercedes 350.

I tried to act normal and complimented him on the house, then true to his word he treated me to lunch.

Arrogant twat!

30

Ballintearly Farm wasn't really a farm. It used to be, but that was many years ago. Now it was a token homage to what it had once been, but all the original buildings were still there, even if they had changed considerably over the years.

Anne lived in the old barn. It had been converted in the nineties when the Irish government had lavished grants on redevelopment during a period of unprecedented boom. Many of the old places had been renovated or extended for bed and breakfast facilities and Ballintearly had made the most of the opportunities. A week hadn't passed without an American or other tourist staying there for a time. There had been an almighty crash in the economy since then but Ballintearly and many of the old farms had benefitted from the government-sponsored windfall.

The barn had been rebuilt from ground up, using all the original materials and now contained anything and everything a home could need for a comfortable lifestyle.

The main farm building had also benefitted from a major upgrade, and Anne's sister and brother-in-law lived a completely separate life from Anne, only crossing paths each Sunday when the extended family would meet for a lavish dinner after church.

Anne wasn't religious. As a Protestant in a

predominantly Catholic country, there were not many options for worship in the little community. But that was good for her. She had not set foot inside a church or chapel since she was a child and had no intention of ever doing so again, at least not until her own funeral. That, she hoped, would not be for a very long time, especially since she now had a new lease of life.

Reinvigorated by the recent meeting with DI Terry McGuire, Anne had felt the cloud of depression lift. Not totally, she knew depression didn't work like that. It was an insidious condition that usually crept up on someone whilst they weren't looking and seemed to steal their soul. It had been quick and dramatic for Anne, no slow decent into the depths of despair. She had crashed almost overnight after the revelation that her colleagues were bent. It was the sense of hopelessness, the knowledge of grave situations beyond her control and the inability to rationalise them. But now she felt better. The bastards would get what was coming to them and all thanks to one brave man back in her homeland of Wales.

She found her car keys in a bowl on a stand by the front door and took her coat from the stair post.

Her ten-year-old Mazda convertible hadn't had a run in over a month; she hadn't felt up to driving, but today she'd take it through the lanes and visit Bray on the east coast, south of Dublin. It wasn't far, the sun was shining and she loved the feeling of the wind blowing through her hair. Her hair was a different colour and much shorter now than it had been when she had bought the car but the sensation would be the same.

She started the engine and put the car in gear. Anne's sister, Julie, had heard the engine turning over and stepped out of her house to check on her. Anne was grateful to Julie, more than she would ever know. Julie and her husband, Niall, had taken her in when she was desperate and had given her space but had been there for her whenever she needed a shoulder to cry on, and it was typical of her big sister to fuss and to check on her. They were similar in most ways, especially physically, until Anne had changed her hairstyle.

Anne waved and smiled and saw Julie's face light up. It was the first time they had both smiled together for far too long.

The Mazda coughed then purred as the underused fuel system began to purge itself and return to what it did best.

* * *

At least the address was out of the way – secluded. He checked the fuel level gauge, he'd have to fill up again before he left Ireland, but at least he wasn't paying.

He pulled the rental car onto the verge and smiled at the attractive brunette woman in the convertible Mazda as it squeezed past him on the narrow road. He thought about the girl on the ferry. She had been a looker and she had seemed amenable to a bit of chitchat. If only he had asked her for her phone number. He cursed himself and he was surprised he had forgotten to ask for it. He had other more pressing things on his mind. He checked his mirror and saw the little drop-top accelerate around the bend he had just travelled. The weather was ideal for the car, he thought; cold, crisp but dry with blue skies.

He put his rental Kia into first gear and pulled off again. The satnav told him he had just under a mile to his destination.

The place wasn't anything like he had expected. The farmhouse was large, an original double-fronted, whitewashed, two-storey with a slate pitched roof, probably built during the middle of the last century and renovated sometime during the last thirty years. Two wings had also been added and a fancy barn conversion occupied the rear of the yard.

The Kia passed the farm gate and pulled into a break in the hedge leading to a fallow field. The driver switched off the engine and pulled his coat from the back seat and his camera from the front.

He walked slowly towards the farm and caught a glimpse of a woman hanging washing on a line near the barn.

Good drying day.

He stood by the gate to the property and the woman looked toward him. She nodded and dropped her washing into a pale blue plastic basket at her feet.

He held up his camera and waved to the woman. "Excuse me... do you mind if I take a few shots?"

The woman frowned and walked towards him. "Sorry?"

"I said, do you mind if I take a few shots? I've been told this is the place my Irish family were born and raised in."

The woman smiled. "Certainly. Help yourself."

"That's a funny accent," he said. "That's not Irish."

The woman shook her head. "It's Welsh. Been here for a while now. Never lose it though," she smiled.

31

Sarah Watkins sat on the wooden decking of her caravan and watched the gulls sweeping down on the remains of a discarded fish-and-chip supper. It annoyed her that some lazy bastards couldn't be bothered to walk a few yards to drop their rubbish in one of the many bins provided on the front. There was no excuse for it.

She sipped her mug of coffee and breathed in the fresh air. She loved the caravan. Her parents had left it to her in their will and she had fond memories of holidaying in Trecco as a child. The place wasn't like it used to be. Trecco was far more 'polished' than when her parents had the van, but she had actually liked the 'tacky' nonsense, the 'Kiss Me Quick' hats, the faggots and peas and sticks of cheap rock that that once been part and parcel of a caravan holiday in Porthcawl. The tack could still be found but the management at the park knew they had to move with the times and were trying their best to offer a better experience for the more discerning holiday maker.

Sarah wrapped her shawl around her shoulders and checked her watch. She was in no hurry but she couldn't get out of the habit of chasing time. It had been her life. As manager of the family transport company, she'd relied on accurate timing. She checked the time against the time on her iPhone. Spot on to the minute.

She knew it was exactly twenty-one minutes past

ten in the morning when the naked man frightened the gulls from their feast and turned to face her and began to play with his erect penis.

32

The call from Anne took me by surprise. She was hysterical.

"Calm down," I said. "Calm down and tell me what's happened."

"It's Julie, my sister," she sobbed. "They got her. She's been attacked."

I was gobsmacked and didn't know what to say. Anne managed to compose herself enough to explain. "This morning, someone came to the farm and attacked her and set fire to the place. It's all gone, Terry. The house is destroyed and Julie is in hospital. She's in intensive care. Someone beat her and left her for dead."

"I'm sorry," Is all I could think of to say. "Are the Garda on the case?"

"Yes, but they don't know where to start."

I was feeling a deep dread in the pit of my stomach. Could it be a coincidence? Unlikely. A couple of days after we speak, her house was torched and her sister put in intensive care.

"Do you think it's them?" she said.

"Why would they attack your sister?"

"To warn me off?"

That thought had crossed my mind. "But they'd go for you, not her."

"That's just it, Terry. We look the same, or at least we did until I changed my hair and dyed it."

"Shit!"

I spent the next ten minutes apologising to Anne for getting her involved and trying to assure her that we'd get whoever was responsible. It didn't make it easier because Anne and I both knew that whoever had carried out the attack on the farm was probably still in Ireland.

I had put her at risk by disclosing my meeting with her when I spoke with Cliff Ambrose. I had done it to flush him out, to glean some evidence, but had not thought at any time that I would be putting Anne at risk. If this attack was as a result of that conversation with Cliff then the investigation had taken a whole new sinister turn.

* * *

WPC Caroline Williams pulled up outside the luxurious caravan on the seafront.

She locked the car and climbed up freshly stained wooden steps to a wide and well-appointed decking area that occupied the side and front of the caravan. She noticed a mug on a wooden coffee table at the front end of the decking and a pair of comfortable looking aluminium recliners.

The door opened before she could knock.

"Mrs Watkins?"

"Sarah, please? I'm not married."

Caroline smiled politely. "Sarah. You called us about a flasher?"

Sarah stepped aside for Caroline to enter and

closed the door behind them.

"Could you tell me what happened?"

"It's like I told the girl on the phone. I was having a coffee on the decking when I saw this naked bloke wanking in front of me."

"Description?"

"About four inches and a little sad looking..."

"I'm sorry?"

Sarah laughed. "Just joking. Got to laugh, haven't you?"

"I suppose so," Caroline said, unsure of herself. She had been expecting someone very upset by the experience but this woman seemed to think it was a joke.

"Did you see his face?"

"I wasn't looking at his face. I was distracted."

"Was he tall, short, dark, fair...?"

"Look, I know you probably think I'm being flippant, but I'm not calling you because he upset me. It really doesn't make a difference to me. I've seen lots of things like that over the years. I'm just worried that some kids might see him. He needs to be stopped. He can't be well in the head."

Caroline took the report and walked down onto the beach to the point where a chip wrapper had been decimated by the gulls. The flasher had been no more than twenty yards from the caravan and Sarah should have been able to get a good look at the man's face. Thankfully, she'd taken a photo of him on her mobile phone. Caroline had checked out the image but it hadn't been in focus. Perhaps Forensics might be able to sharpen the image? She heard the bell from her own phone to announce that Sarah had forwarded the image to her.

* * *

The Kia drove down the ramp and off the ferry at Fishguard.

Job done, the driver took the new by-pass and stopped for a pint in Red Roses en route to his rental property in Carmarthen. The house had not had a tenant for nearly a year, but he didn't mind. He had made the most of the place during that time. It was great to escape the bustle of Cardiff.

It had all gone surprisingly easy. He had been worried he wouldn't find the woman but the address and description he had been given were spot on.

There was no reward for the job, other than the peace of mind that a threat to their liberty had been removed. That was good enough for him. No one would ever connect him to the attack in Ireland; they'd know the reason for it but never join the dots. After all, the eyes of the law were firmly fixed in one small area. This would throw the cat amongst the pigeons.

33

Monday morning. I had a conference with Ron and Dai. The attack in Ireland had changed the profile of the case considerably. We were now racing against the clock because I was now absolutely sure Cliff knew we were on to him. I wondered about the CCTV at his place. Had he caught me on the recording?

At least Anne was safe. A quick chat with the Garda and she was whisked off to one of their safe houses for a while. I was confident she'd be okay. No one did safe houses better than the Garda. Let's face it, they'd had enough practice.

"How are the financials looking, Dai?" Ron asked glumly. I could see this was eating at him. It's not easy to accept that one of your own is a possible killer.

"Well, put it this way, the three dickheads used to spend more than they earned during their squad days. And as for Cliff, well, I think he should have been an investment banker. No idea where he's getting it all from."

"They've been at it, big time for years and are still at it," I said. "Chief, I need four warrants; can we have another conference with the CPS?"

Ron looked down at his desk and seemed lost in his thoughts for a moment. "Fuck it," he finally said. "Let's do it. I'll fix it for two o'clock, and don't go off the deep end this time, Terry."

"Well, make sure you get a good 'un from the CPS this time," I sniped.

Two o'clock arrived and the CPS solicitor was waiting for me. It was that bloody Reginald Archer again. He was dressed in his usual black leather overcoat, blue pinstripe suit. He looked like that German officer from 'Allo, Allo'... what's his name... Von Klomp? I spread my cards on the table and Reg started tutting.

I was thinking it had all gone to rat shit again.

Then I threw my low-baller into the mix. "I've received information from a reliable source that the body of Billy was kept in a freezer at the home of DCI Ambrose," I lied.

Archer didn't look convinced. "How reliable?"

"One hundred per cent," I said slowly. "I can stake my life on it."

Archer nodded. "In that case, crack on DI McGuire, you have my authority to swear out warrants. Murder for Ambrose, conspiracy to murder for the other three."

I was elated and I tasked Dai with arranging a special court so I could swear out the warrants. We were off and running.

34

I had no problem getting the warrants, the magistrates clerk, another one of the old school, Major J. L. Davies got them signed and wished me happy hunting. I had great respect for him. He'd served in the Army and had won the Military Medal at Goose Green, taking out an Argentinian machine gun nest. He knew what loyalty meant and was clearly disturbed by the proceedings. "Inspector," he said to me in private, "Put them away for a long time. They are a disgrace to the Force and their colleagues and I will not tolerate such disgraceful acts."

I called another conference for 5am and assembled four teams, all handpicked detectives and SOC Officers from all over the Force. I gave them the background to the operation and I laid it all on the line for them. The look of horror on their faces was to be expected, but I knew they'd do what was right.

"I want two officers doing the arrests and two doing the premises' search. We're looking for the following items," I said. "A double-edge serrated knife, nylon rope, heavy duty polythene, any type of acid, bank statements, cash and probably drugs. This lot have been at it for years. Three have retired and one is still a serving officer. Remember, they are to make no phone calls upon arrest. Also, the cadaver dog will be attending at the home of DCI Ambrose. They all live within the Force area. You have your packages, the strike will be at 6am and your prisoners will be taken to designated stations. Now get to it and bring me home the bacon."

Ron and I sat nervously in the command room whilst the teams went about their business. I would have liked to go too but because of my connection with Cliff, Ron insisted I stayed well clear.

* * *

It was 5:50am and John Fuller was my eyes and ears in the raids on the retired detective constables. Dai Williams would do the job for me at Ambrose's gaff. An inspector from Complaints and Discipline, a guy called Peter Chapman, was leading the raid of DC Stevens' place. A regional carrier unit was also in attendance and because of the mention of firearms, the Firearms Tactical Unit was also chaffing at the bit.

* * *

Stevens' house was a well-presented semi-detached house, one of four in a rural lane off the main drag between Bridgend and Pencoed. He had clearly been spending time in the garden since he retired. The flower beds were neat and ready for the spring flowers and the lawn was one of those Astroturf jobbies that cost a fortune and look perfect all year round.

John and the inspector had organised the raid team and they waited patiently for the signal to go.

One of the support officers, fully kitted in Kevlar

vest and helmet, smashed the front door off its hinges with a dirty great big ram and the raid was on.

Simultaneously, another team was doing the same at the homes of James and Green and Dai Williams was waiting for the signal to go. Ambrose would be the last hit and it all depended on the others being home.

About 6:15am, the first call came in. Stevens had been arrested. Then at short intervals, Green and James were also arrested.

* * *

Dai Williams grinned as Cliff Ambrose opened the door. He produced his warrant card and thrust it in Ambrose's face. "Detective Sergeant Williams," he said.

"I know who you are. You're Terry's lapdog."

Dai bristled but didn't let it show. He produced the warrant and barged past Ambrose.

"You're making a big mistake, lad," Ambrose said. "This will fuck up your career... big time."

"Not half as much as your career is about to get fucked up," Dai laughed.

* * *

The call came from Dai to inform me that Cliff Ambrose was in custody. I turned to Ron. "That was the easy part, Chief, now the work begins. I want one of those bastards to crack and blow it wide open."

35

Up to the Big House again to seek permission to go for Chris Coulter. The ACC, Ron, John, Dai and me, and my favourite CPS, Andrea Edwards, were assembled. I was confident that Andrea could do the business for us; she had advised me on many a tricky case. She had just returned from maternity leave and this was her first big one since her return, not a bad starter for ten or as in Coulter's case; I hoped it would be twenty to thirty – years, that is.

Andrea smiled at me as the others chatted amongst themselves. I smiled back. She looked tired but good. Her wavy red hair was tied back from her face and her lipstick matched her hair. Her green dress looked good with her colouring and a pair of thin-framed spectacles was edged in the same colour as the dress. I knew from my experience with Molly and my own kids that motherhood didn't always turn out the way you expect it to but Andrea seemed to be at peace, happy with herself and that was good to see. She was as sharp as a scalpel and had studied law at Jesus College, Oxford. She had once told me that she was lucky. She had been born into a wealthy family. Her mother was a surgeon and could afford the thirty grand a year course fees and the extortionate living costs on top. I really liked Andrea because she understood that the luck of birth could and often did determine fate, and that was something she was trying to change for some. She had set up a charity that she heavily subsidised to provide funding for bright kids who couldn't afford the fees of Oxbridge. "A cracker this, Terry," she said.

"Aren't they always?" I nodded.

"Have you got enough?"

"Yes, Andrea." I laid it all out for her. She sat with a straight back as I began. The others in the room stopped chatting and listened intently.

"Not sure about the witnesses," Andrea grimaced as she scanned a page of antecedents on Vic and Sams.

"I know the witnesses are all from the 'dark side', but I believe them all and I'm sure a jury will too."

We were there for the best part of three hours, going through the statements and other documents.

Andrea concentrated on Coulter's file and the information we had gathered. Finally, after I was just about to lose the will to live, she took a sharp intake of breath and smiled, "Go for him, Terry. Sounds like an evil bastard... The Fox eh? Well, hunt the bastard down. As for the rape, I think we have enough with the statements, but if his DNA is a match as well that will do it for the jury."

I thanked Andrea and she stood and kissed me on the cheek. I collected all the evidence and we were away. The hounds were baying, and the fox was fucked.

John and I returned to the office and started ringing around. I wanted to assemble a team of about ten. Scene of Crime Officers, Firearms, Search Team, the whole shooting match. We'd give Coulter the old 'six o'clock knock.' Although I knew I could arrest Coulter and search his home under the Police and Criminal Evidence Act, what was commonly known as PACE within the legal profession, I decided to play it safe and arrange for a warrant to be sworn, just in case he wasn't at home. The briefing was arranged for 5am.

36

My team arrived dead on time. Once more they had not been told what the operation entailed but it wouldn't take a genius to work it out after the recent raids on the other bent coppers. When I told them there were a few inevitable sighs and groans.

A voice from the back of the group shouted. "Always thought he was bent, boss. Hope you've got enough on him."

"Oh aye, we've got enough, and I think what we have is only the tip of the iceberg."

I filled them all in and tasked them with their duties at the house. Now, having heard my briefing on Coulter and his nefarious antics, they were all chomping at the bit.

"Leave Coulter to me," I warned them. "I'll hook him away and leave you all with a free run; turn his place upside down," I said grimly.

We arrived at Coulter's home. It was nothing special, three-bedroom detached, nice part of town with a local library and a huddle of small shops. I knocked the door and a few minutes later, Coulter appeared. He was wearing a red silk dressing gown and leather slippers. I noticed an overnight case in the hallway behind him.

I identified myself but I knew he recognised me. I had never worked with him but I'd seen him a few times in briefings for Royal visits and other events that needed a gathering of coppers from across the force area. "Chris Coulter, you are under arrest for the possession and supply of Class A drugs, firearms offences, and perverting the course of justice," I cautioned him, but he said nothing. I saw his bottom lip tremble and I watched the colour drain from his face as he began to cry. It was a strange reaction for such a ruthless twat and a reaction that left me disappointed. I wanted him to cut up rough, to swing for me so I could swing back. I dearly wanted to smash his bloody face in.

"Cuff him and take him down the nick," I told Bailey who was eagerly brandishing handcuffs. I watched Coulter walk away with Roger. I expected a bit more of a fight, I expected him to be screaming for a brief and all that kind of shit, but nothing. There was always a first time for everything.

As I was about to leave and let the others get on with the job, I remembered the holdall in the hallway. I checked it out and found some overnight things, wash bag, pyjamas and a car rental agreement. There was also a small paper receipt. I held it close to my face to read the small print and began to smile.

I left the team to go about their business and fixed a conference for 2pm.

Back at the nick, I put the piece of shit in front of the custody sergeant and presented the reasons for the arrest. Coulter was 'detained pending further enquiries'.

37

My team was assembled in the incident room and all
were in buoyant mood, which surprised me. I honestly
thought most would have problems with arresting one
of their own, but it seemed they were all just as pissed
about the corruption as I was. That was extremely
satisfying and raised my spirits. Had they been
awkward, it wouldn't have mattered to me, not really, I
knew we were doing the right thing, how could we do
anything else? Corruption is a cancer. It has to be cut out
before it spreads. My only worry was how far it might
have spread already.

"Right, what have we got? Make my day," I asked
the team.

My top SOC man, DS Glyn Walcott, stepped
forward. "Boss, we've got about a kilo of coke that we
found in the frame of an old bicycle, a Smith and Wesson
handgun with numbers filed off that was in a bag in a
hole under his garden shed and a diary with dates and
cash amounts going back donkey's years. Also, I would
estimate about a hundred grand in cash."

That surprised me, too. "Well done, all of you.
Many thanks."

I spoke to Glyn, "Once I get all the necessary swabs,
will you liaise with the lab? I need that rape comparison,
like yesterday. It's important."

Glyn nodded. "No problem, boss. Leave it to me."

I went back to the custody suite. Coulter had been banged up.

The sergeant was a young officer. Probably no more than six or seven years' service, that was young in comparison to me.

"Has he requested a brief, Sarge?"

"Aye, that shyster, Roderick Hughes. He'll be here within the hour. He's been in court."

"Give me a shout when he arrives, I'll bring him up to speed."

It was exactly an hour later when I got the call and went back to the custody suite. Hughes was there, a rather rotund individual who sweats for Wales. He was a typical villain's brief, no moral fortitude, a blood-sucking parasite. I hated him with a passion, not because of his job, I understood the need for good defence briefs, but Rod was just a dislikeable character. He seemed to relish winding up police officers.

"What have you got, Inspector? I hope it's sound," he said. "I'll be making representation for my client to be released," he blustered.

"Aye, whatever floats your boat, Rod," I snapped, "but he's not going anywhere, only down the fucking Suwannee for a long voyage, unless he plays ball. Now you go and have a chat with him. He's screwed on what we've found up at his house."

I took the solicitor into the interview room where all the exhibits recovered from the house were laid out. "Let's see him explain this lot away."

It was time for a cup of coffee. The brief would need some time to take instructions. I couldn't imagine him being too quick. It would take him weeks to invent some plausible excuse for all that shit.

38

I had sunk three coffees by the time I got the call from the Custody Sergeant and made my way to the interview room.

Coulter appeared with Rod and was flanked by two uniform officers. The solicitor was looking his usual cocky self.

"Inspector, I have advised my client to say nothing throughout any scheduled interviews," he said.

I knew they were playing for time. No reply to questions left them open to construct a load of shit later on. At least the change in disclosure rules of courts meant that the jury would be aware that he had made no reply and then could read into it whatever they wanted to.

I was still left annoyed. "Rod, can I say something off the record?"

Rod looked interested. "Go ahead, Inspector."

I stepped up close to Rod, right in his personal space. "I don't give a damn if he stays mute for the rest of his days. He's fucked and I'll make sure he does time for his actions. Now, can we please get down to business?" I knew I was being overbearing but it was the only thing that seemed to make a difference with Rod. He liked to be in control and to bully officers with what he believed was his superior knowledge, but he had to know it wouldn't work on me.

I looked at Coulter, he was still a bit peaky and eyeing the exhibits. At least he'd stopped crying. I hated to see a grown man cry, especially a bent bastard like this one.

I went through the usual shite before the interview: introducing myself and getting those present to do the same for the benefit of the recording. Then I was ready.

"You've been arrested for numerous alleged offences. I wish to start with the rape allegation.

"A woman by the name of Amanda Keller was eighteen when you were on plain clothes duties down on the Bay in Cardiff. She alleged you raped her, what have you got to say to that?"

Coulter looked scared but managed, "No comment."

"Do you know Amanda Keller?"

"No comment."

I was undeterred. I had to go through the motions. "She alleges you raped her in the lane opposite The Packet pub. You beat her and threatened to kill her if she reported you."

"No comment."

"The exhibits and swabs are still with us. When they're examined will your DNA be on them?"

Now Coulter looked unsure but remained defiant. "No comment."

I was used to this, it was bread and butter for any investigator but I still sighed. "I'm giving you the opportunity to negate this allegation."

"No comment."

"Do you know a pimp by the name of Phil Asher?"

"No comment."

"Well, he was pimping Amanda at the time and he says that he gave you five-hundred-quid cash from compensation money that Amanda received a few months later."

"No comment."

"Let's move on. Do you know these men, Victor Thomas, Peter Samuels, Lloyd Cove, Steve Diamond and Elwyn Fowler?"

"No comment."

"These men are making serious allegations against you of corruption, drug supplying and possession of firearms. In fact, Thomas and Samuels have spent many a year behind bars as a result of your dealings with them."

"No comment."

Coulter then turned to Rod.' "Have I got to listen to this shit? Fucking load of old lags, they are."

I seized the chance. "I take it by that comment you do know them?"

Coulter realised his error. "No comment."

"Is there any point in revealing all their allegations?" I asked.

"No comment."

"Okay, we'll let the jury decide if they are telling the truth or not."

I then drew Coulter's attention to the exhibits; the gun, the drugs, the cash and the diary.

"What have you got to say about this lot found in your home this morning?"

"No comment."

"I find it to be stretching the realms of coincidence that the offences you have been arrested for just happen to be the same as the exhibits would suggest."

Coulter snapped. "You bastards! You planted that lot."

"That's the pot calling the kettle black," I said calmly. "Can you explain them, please?"

"No comment."

"Is there any point in talking to you any further? We have all the statements and with this little lot, I do believe you have had your chips."

"No comment."

"Just one more thing," I said. "I found a holdall in your hallway this morning. It contained overnight items and a car hire agreement and a receipt for diesel from a garage in a place outside of Dublin. Have you been to Ireland over the last few days?"

Coulter's face turned red and he pulled at the collar of his shirt. "No comment."

I smiled, because I knew he was screwed. "I've enjoyed our little chat. We'll have another one tomorrow as soon as I have the DNA results and have spoken to the Garda. I'm sure we'll be able to get some video eyes on your car on the ferry and many other points in Ireland."

I told the two officers standing at the rear of the

interview room to take him back to his cell.

I then conferred with the custody sergeant and completed all the necessary documentation.

I walked with Rod to the main door, and he stopped to speak. "Inspector, I think he's well and truly fucked. Good night." As he left through the door he added, "Oh, I'm in court all day tomorrow. If you need to interview him, give the office a ring and they'll send a legal rep up. Got to be seen to be doing something, obviously."

That surprised me. It wasn't a reaction I would have expected from Rod, but it made me feel good. I retired to my office with a big grin and got stuck into the malt.

Tomorrow was another day and it was going to be busy.

39

I was in the office, bright-eyed and bushy-tailed, when Glyn Walcott burst in like a child with a voucher for a sweet shop.

"Boss? He's fucked! The Garda confirmed his car in several places en route to the farmhouse in Ireland and the woman at the car hire place in Swansea confirmed he hired a car from them. The Garda checked the petrol station near Dublin and confirmed the receipt was for thirty litres of diesel on the same day the farmhouse was torched and Anne's sister was attacked. But that's not all. DNA on the swabs and clothing from the Amanda rape belong to him, it's his semen, and his prints are all over the pack of drugs."

"Brilliant, Glyn. Brilliant. It looks to me like Ambrose and Coulter are joined at the hip in this crap. We can now tie them both into the same pool of shit. Let's see what the bastard has to say about that."

Glyn frowned "Oh, there's something else, boss..."

I felt a dread.

"His prints are on the gun as well, thought I would just keep that one back," he grinned at last.

I punched him on the arm.

I rang the custody suite, told them I wanted to interview Coulter and that they needed to get his legal rep. Within half an hour, I got the call.

I sprang down to the charge room and, lo and

behold, his rep was none other than an old ex-colleague, Bob Pengers. Bob had been a cracking copper, had about 15 years in when he fell foul of a certain senior officer who hounded him out of the service. That senior officer cost us a good copper. I shook Bob's hand.

"It's The Fox, is it?" he sighed. "Always knew he was at it, do the business on him, Terry. You've got enough evidence, so Rod-the-Sod tells me."

"I only want to put to him the trip to Ireland and the additional evidence regarding the rape, Bob, then I'll charge and remand the arsehole."

"Carry on, Inspector," he said, with a wry smile and chuckle.

Ten minutes later, I interviewed Coulter.

"I'll keep this short and to the point," I said. I struggled to keep a smug expression off my face. "Regarding the alleged rape, your DNA is everywhere on the girl's clothing, your semen is everywhere. Your prints are on the gun and drugs recovered at your home. Have you anything to say, any explanations?"

"No comment."

"What can you tell me about Ireland?"

"No comment."

"You hired a car and drove across to Ireland, using the Fishguard-to-Rosslaire ferry and then travelled to the home of a former South Wales detective and seriously assaulted her sister and torched the place."

Coulter's face was a picture when I mentioned Anne's sister. That was news to him. He must have mistaken her for Anne and had no idea up to that point that he had got the wrong woman.

"That's right. Our witness from Ireland is safe and will come to court to give evidence."

He stared at the floor. "No comment."

"I'll ask you for the last time, have you anything to say regarding all the allegations?"

"No comment."

I was sick of the sight of him and Coulter was bundled back in his cell.

Me and Bob walked together back to the custody suite and Bob told me he didn't need to be present for the charging. It was a formality.

As I accompanied Bob to the exit door I wondered if he'd be in my position if he'd stayed in the job. I believed he would have and I felt sad and angry that we had lost him to a vindictive personality clash.

40

I gave the ACC a call, just to keep him up to speed. He wanted to put out a press release before the remand. John had already formulated the charges after liaising with the CPS, so I faxed him a copy. He was over the moon with the result.

I charged Coulter with the rape of Amanda Keller, possession and supplying of Class A drugs, unlawful possession of a Section 1 firearm, and perverting the course of justice. After the caution, guess what? He made no reply. I hadn't done anything with the incident in Ireland. The Garda would need to deal with that as a separate nail in his coffin as it was committed on Irish soil. The following morning, he was remanded in custody to await trial.

I was delighted and angry at the outcome; delighted we had caught him but angry that one of our own had committed such appalling crimes. But there was something else niggling at the back of my mind and that was the diary. Why keep a diary going back years? Anyway, I had to keep that on the back burner because I had a gut feeling that the lifer Steve Diamond could help me out with that. All I had to do was get him nearer home, but that was for the future. I also wondered whether Coulter would eventually accept he was screwed and plead guilty.

* * *

Caroline, the young policewoman, entered my office with several sheets of paper. "Excuse me, sir, I know you're up to your eyes in things, but I'd like you to take a look at these."

She laid a series of poor resolution photos on the desk. I didn't need to ask what they were, it was pretty bloody obvious.

"I tried to get the techies to enhance the image of his face but I'm not sure it's good enough," she said.

"I agree. No way you could get an ID to stick in court. Do you know who it is?" The face looked familiar but I couldn't place it.

She shook her head.

"Don't worry," I smiled. "You've done well. We can only do so much. With cases like this sometimes we just have to wait. He'll cock up one day... excuse the pun."

Caroline laughed but I could see she was disappointed.

"I've been thinking about your request for an aide."

She looked glum. I knew she was hoping to bring the flasher to book, but I was also a realist and knew it wasn't always that simple. "I've got a spot for you. You can work with DC Roger Bailey for a while and then we'll see how you get on."

Her smile was heart-warming.

One of the great things about being in my position was the ability to help new officers to develop their careers. I was a great believer in instilling the true values of a proper detective. I hoped that I'd have some influence on her career, an influence that would always keep her safe and away from the 'dark side.'

41

I had already picked my interviewers, teams of two – the best in the Force, in my opinion. I knew we would need the best because I had an idea all the suspects would be saying nothing.

Me and Dai would interview Cliff Ambrose.

Prior to the interviews, at 4pm, I called all the teams together. The searches had been completed. Large amounts of cash and drugs had been recovered from the ex-detectives' homes. A good result, but Ambrose's home revealed the most. Cash, drugs, what we believed was the knife, pieces of polythene, acid, the blonde hairs; and the cadaver dog had headed straight to the freezer. All in all a cracking result, but I wanted more. I wanted Billy's killer, and I was determined to get him.

We started interviewing Ambrose at 6pm. After going through the formalities, bearing in mind the arrogant bastard didn't want a brief, I hit him with the first question.

"Did you kill Billy Hughes?"

Leaning back on his chair, hands behind head, he said, "That's for you to prove, Terry. That's for you to prove." I couldn't believe it, this scumbag was taking the piss for the benefit of the tape recording.

I felt sick to my stomach; the enormity of the case suddenly hit me. I had to hold it together. I wanted to lean across the table and smash the arrogant fuck in the face. "This is what I think happened," I said, as calmly as I could. "Billy got the hump because you were ripping him off with the informant's money. He confronted you in the caravan and you just stabbed him to death. Is that what happened, Cliff?"

"Nice story, Terry, and that's all it is."

"We'll see, Cliff. I'm sure your old buddies don't want to be done for murder. One of them will crack. Oh, by the way, as we speak, the knife is being tested for DNA, bit silly keeping it, but there we are, you've always been an arrogant prick."

"Arrogant? Yes, Terry, but not a loser like you."

I grinned. "Have you ever worked with former DI Chris Coulter?"

"I'm sure you already know the answer. I worked with lots of coppers over the years. Most of them wouldn't try and stitch up mates."

I could see it in his eyes, he was thinking, trying to work out what we had.

Interview terminated – for a while.

I called another conference at 10 pm. I was getting sick of them but I kept reminding myself they were vital to keep the team briefed. All three other interviews went as expected: 'No comment.' So, we were no further on. All to be expected, really. They knew the score.

I called a halt, then told all the team to go home and get some kip and come back in the morning, fresh. Hopefully, I'd have the DNA results on the knife and hair, also 'cut comparisons' on the polythene. Then we could really go to town.

42

I didn't want to do another interview with the suspects until I had the DNA results.

At 10am, the lab called through to the office. "You have positive matches on everything, Terry. The blood on the knife and hairs from the freezer are Billy's. Polythene cuts match the knife. You've got a result."

I sat quietly for a moment and allowed myself a big grin.

The team gathered together whilst I briefed them on the next series of interviews. It was imperative that we were all singing from the same hymn sheet.

"Disclose the lot to those three bent bastards and tell them they'll all be charged with the murder of Billy Hughes. Tell them that, nothing else. Then leave them to sweat. The clock is ticking, boys. Go and do the business."

Within the hour, my teams were ringing me. "You got them, boss. They'll tell us everything, but they didn't do Billy. It was Ambrose, and it was all over the informant's money. They torched the van and disposed of the body, all on the instructions of Ambrose. They were in too deep to tell him to fuck off."

"Brilliant! Get me a transcript from one of them and get it to me as soon as possible."

I got the transcript off the interview with Stevens. I read it and then me and Dai went back in with Cliff.

"Well, Cliff. The three of them cracked and have put the finger on you for Billy. You are in deep shit, butt. I think you better get a brief."

"Listen, Terry, don't tell me what I need," he fumed, his face flushing red. "What deal have you offered the three pricks?"

"That's for me to know, and you to guess, you arrogant son of a bitch."

He finally looked worried. "What can you do for me, Terry, for old times' sake?"

This was a new and unexpected turn. "What are you offering, Cliff?"

He thought for a moment. "Look, it was self-defence. Billy wanted me to meet him at his caravan down in Trecco Bay. I took my lads with me, just in case he got shirty. He was ranting and raving about how he thought I was screwing him over and he came at me with the knife. The boys were outside. Billy was high as a kite, as normal. He lunged at me, we struggled on the floor. I took the knife off him and just let him have it."

"Let him have it? He was about eight stone soaking wet. Why stab him?"

Cliff's arrogance couldn't be contained, not even when his life depended on it. "He was a bottom feeder," he said, "lowest of the low. I had a nice scam going with him, 'til he got fucking shirty. He deserved it, the little twat."

"How many times did you stab him?"

He shrugged. "Three times. I think he'd gone after

the first, to be honest."

"What happened then?"

"Well, there was a bit of blood, so I called the boys. They were fucking gobsmacked, ranting and raving and running around like headless chickens.

"The polythene roll and the rope was there. Billy had been using it to cover a leak in the caravan roof, so I just wrapped Billy up tight and then we put him in Billy's van. I was going to bury him then and there on the dunes, but I didn't have a spade. So we took him up to my place and put him in my freezer. Before we left, I torched the caravan. It was on its axles in minutes. Have you seen one go up, Tel?" he grinned smugly.

I was thinking he might have come out of this better if he'd burnt the body in the caravan. It could have got so damaged that we'd never have discovered the truth. I was just thankful he wasn't as smart as he'd always thought he was. But I was still shocked by the extent of his arrogance. "It's all so matter of fact for you, Cliff. Have you no conscience?"

"Look, Terry. I've dealt with druggies all over Europe, butt. Freezer, iced lakes, incineration, nobody gives a fuck about them... oh, sorry, you do," he said in a flippant manner. "I knew you wouldn't let it go, like a dog with a fucking bone."

"Yes, but why bury him now, after all this time?"

"Selling up, butt. Had a cracking offer on the house. Time for Billy to go, I thought. Fucking trouble is, didn't bury him deep enough, did I? Thought if anybody did find him the police would think it was a gangland killing."

"What about all the money, all the trappings of wealth, what's all that about, why so obvious?"

"Status, Terry," Cliff sniffed. "You think it's corrupt over here? Go to Europe, butt, and make your fortune. That's what I did and no one's the wiser, my friend."

I shook my head. "I'm no friend of yours."

Cliff shrugged as if it didn't matter to him one way or another. "What's the deal, then?"

I was furious. "You want a fucking deal? About twenty-odd years, I hope. Interview terminated. Dai, get this piece of shit out of my sight."

43

After all the interviews were completed, I arranged for all four prisoners to be housed at Bridgend Bridewell to be formally charged. The Bridewell was a self-contained two-storey building situated on Queen Street on the Bridgend Industrial Estate. It wasn't a 'real' police station where members of the public could report crimes or produce vehicle documents for checking. It was a purpose-built facility serving the entire Force and was a centralised specialist custody centre. The building was totally secure with the obligatory identification passes needed to enter. The passes were only issued to police personnel. A key pad call system at the entrance identified the different departments and allowed members of the public to press and call for whatever department they wanted and they would then be let into a reception area.

The custody suite occupied the ground floor, with approximately sixty cells with two custody sergeants. Two banks of interview rooms were also available and were managed by the hub personnel who interviewed suspects in custody.

The first floor was split into separate offices. The main office was open plan and housed the CID, traffic officers, response officers and the bail team. The space was also occupied by admin staff and the duty inspector. I had seen as many as thirty officers in there at one time.

Computers, telephones, radios and other up-to-date equipment were available for the officers and helped to speed up the processing of prisoners – in theory. There were also separate offices for the chief superintendent and senior management team. Other rooms housed the Priority Policing Team, Intel, Financial Investigations officers and even more administration staff.

All the interview rooms had audio and CCTV recording, which had become commonplace.

CCTV also covered the whole site. Vehicle access was via a one-way system that was strictly controlled through the IN and OUT gates.

I found the place depressing and very clinical. All the windows were tinted and coated with some high-tech stuff that made them impenetrable.

Prior to shipping them off to the Bridewell, I conferred with my old 'friend' at the CPS, Reg Archer. Fair play, the first thing he did was shake my hand. "Well done, Inspector. Now let's formulate some charges for the bastards. Ambrose will be done for murder, possession and conspiracy to supply Class A drugs, and money laundering. Stevens, Green and James for possession and conspiracy to supply Class A drugs, and perverting the course of justice. Do you agree with that?"

"No problem," I said. "I think Ambrose will plead self-defence with Billy, so we'll use those three other bastards for the prosecution. Let a jury decide."

"A job well done, Inspector. It's been a pleasure... oh, and by the way, that informant of yours, the one who tipped you off about the hairs in the freezer? Give him a pat on the back from me," he winked.

Next stop, the custody suite.

I charged Stevens, Green and James with various offences and, as expected, they made no reply.

I charged Ambrose in his cell, because he decided to play silly buggers and wouldn't come out. I could have forced the issue – I'd have loved to lay into the twat – but there wasn't any point. Perhaps that's what he wanted me to do so that he could discredit the case and me. I wasn't going to play into his hands.

After charging, he actually said that he was glad it was me that brought him to book. Can you bloody believe that? He then offered me his hand to shake. I was sickened. I just turned and slammed the cell door.

A special court was convened the next day. They were all remanded in custody for trial.

I took a walk through the shopping centre in Bridgend. I needed a break from it all and idly stared at the electrical goods in one of the shops. The fancy toaster like the one Cliff had in his kitchen was on display. £110 for a toaster? *Twat!*

I eventually returned to the station and gathered all the team before we retired to the lounge bar of the Castle Hotel for me to buy them all a few beers – expensive job being a DI. I thanked them all for a job well done. I hoped they would never have to deal with anything like that again.

44

It didn't take me and John long to prepare the file for the CPS; and after a few conferences, their barrister decided to formulate a few more minor charges for the indictment; the more the merrier, as far as I was concerned.

Within a few months, the case had been listed for trial – for two weeks, because at the plea hearing, yup, as expected, Ambrose pleaded not guilty.

In the meantime, I had John speak to all the witnesses and ensure that they were all still up for it. They were, which was a big relief. Some cases had gone wonky on me at a late stage and messed the whole thing up.

Out of the blue, the day before the trial, Bob Pengers gave me a bell and the heads up. "Terry, this twat... The Fox? He's intimating pleading to the first four, the rape etc, if the rest are left on the file. This is between you and me. They are going to try it on the morning because they think some of the witnesses will shit out."

"Cheers, Bob. I owe you one."

The day of the trial arrived. Me and John got there early with all the exhibits; we spread them out in the court. Then the usher secured the doors.

We caught a cup of shitty vending machine brown water that was criminally labelled as coffee and then waited for the witnesses to arrive. Fair play, in they walked, one by one, all the prosecution witnesses, brilliant.

I got John to look after them down in the canteen, until they were needed.

I went into court, told the prosecution barrister the good news that all my witnesses were present and stood back to enjoy the next bit of the show.

Our barrister had a chat with the defence version. Then I got what I'd been hoping for.

The prosecution brief called me over. "Detective Inspector? He will plead to the first four counts, if the rest are left on file."

"Well," I said. "I don't know about that, sir. He deserves all he gets."

"Inspector, he is going to get the same, trust me."

"As long as you guarantee that, sir. I'll go along with it."

"All rise!" the usher shouted as Judge Justice Watkin-Evans shuffled into court. We all bowed and he asked the bailiff to bring the prisoner up to the dock.

Coulter, cuffed to two burly wardens, didn't look too good. He stood, and the clerk read the charges to him. As expected, he entered a guilty plea to the first four charges and 'not guilty' to the other four, then he slumped into the chair provided for him in the dock.

Both barristers did their fancy performance and had their say; the judge listened intently. Once they finished, the judge ordered Coulter to stand.

"You have pleaded guilty to four very serious charges. I am mindful that by doing so, you have saved this court time and yourself some embarrassment. However, you were a serving police officer and you used the office to your own end. You forcibly beat and raped a young vulnerable girl. You have supplied drugs and firearms to criminals. Quite frankly, you are a disgrace."

The judge paused a moment whilst he began jotting notes. "Count one... ten years. Count two... five years. Count three... five years and count four... five years. That's a total of twenty-five years. Take him down."

Coulter was shocked. I think he must have expected some lesser outcome, but I was delighted.

"I would like to commend Detective Inspector McGuire and his team for bringing this man to book," the judge announced. "They are a credit to their police force and to the people of South Wales."

The judge stood and the usher signalled for everyone else to do the same before the judge made his dramatic exit.

I made my way to the canteen and broke the news to John and the witnesses.

"We knew you'd do the business, Terry. Cheers, mate," Victor said.

Me and John left the happy crowd to finish their drinks and made our way back to the office.

I opened the malt and we toasted the witnesses. My time with John had come to an end, but I suspected this wouldn't be the last time we would work together.

I rang Molly and told her I was on my way home. It was only 3pm. That was a rare event for me.

45

Three months on from the day I charged the other four corrupt bastards, they all appeared at Cardiff Crown Court for the plea.

Stevens, Green and James all pleaded guilty to all charges. Ambrose pleaded not guilty. I looked at him and he smiled at me – *still an arrogant bastard.*

The judge, Justice Watkin-Evans, adjourned the case for a week so that the trial of Ambrose could begin.

A few days later, I received a call from the prison. Ambrose wanted to see me.

I paid him a visit the following day. He was dressed in prison clothes and looked pretty sorry for himself in the interview room.

I had no time for the bastard but I wanted to hear what he had to say. "What do you want, Cliff?"

"Will you say a few words in mitigation? I've been advised to plead. That Watkin-Evans is a bad bastard when it comes to sentencing. My brief says I may pull a fifteen stretch on a plea."

"Whatever, Cliff, whatever," I said. I just wanted it to end, to put it all behind me and move on.

Whilst I waited for the trial to begin, life went on as normal. There was always crime to deal with and there was always someone who needed help as a result of those crimes; and the flasher was still running around the caravan park.

I tried to take it easy, to go through the motions and

let Dai and the others sort things out. Caroline was working well with DC Bailey and looked like she would be a valuable asset to the department. She was still annoyed that she hadn't had any luck with the flasher, though.

The day of the trial finally arrived and the four defendants were back in the dock. The charges were put to Ambrose and he pleaded guilty.

Before sentence, his brief called me to the witness box. "I understand, Detective Inspector McGuire, you wish to say a few words about my client?"

"Yes, sir, I do." I waited a moment to ensure the whole court was listening. "I felt it was only right to come here and say a few words about a man who had been a fellow officer, a man who, like me, swore to uphold the law without fear or favour. I felt it was my duty to do so. So here I am, fulfilling that duty," I paused for effect and I could see I was beginning to try the patience of the old judge. I cleared my throat. "The man is a disgrace to the police force, your Honour! He has let his colleagues down and to be honest, I detest him, he makes my skin crawl." I turned to the defence barrister. "Is that what you expected, sir?"

The brief looked shocked and then sat down, speechless.

Justice Watkin-Evans spoke. "Will you all please stand?" Then, in a severe voice – a tone of voice only court judges seemed to possess – he began his sentencing.

"Stevens, Green and James, you have pleaded guilty... and in view of the betrayal of your office and the public you were sworn to serve, I have no option other than to pass a substantial custodial sentence," he too paused for effect. "I sentence you all to eighteen years' imprisonment. Officers take them down."

He waited for the court officers to remove the shell-shocked ex-coppers from the court before he addressed Ambrose. "As for you, Ambrose, it is quite obvious that you are a devious, manipulative individual with no scruples. You have made vast amounts of money from your criminal activities, culminating in the death of a human being. You will go to prison for life, and you will serve a minimum of twenty-six years. Take him down."

Ambrose finally cracked, but not as I would have expected. He laughed, raucous, guffaws of laughter that sent shivers down my spine as the court officers dragged him away to the cells.

The judge was clearly disturbed by Ambrose's outburst, too. He gathered his composure then looked across at me in the witness box. "Detective Inspector McGuire, you and your team are a credit to the police force. To investigate colleagues cannot be easy. I commend you all and, by the way, I concur with your earlier comments about that ghastly man, Ambrose. I see many cases presented at this court and I am never so saddened than when I hear of police officers betraying the trust of the public they are employed to protect. Thankfully, there are officers who will always stand up against such corruption and ensure these criminals are brought to justice." He paused. "Case closed."

I sat in the court until everyone had left and stared at the Court of Arms above the judge's grand chair. It was a symbol of authority, a reminder to all in the court that we all answered to a higher power – whatever that was – and that no man was above the law. I knew some liked to think they were untouchable, but Karma had a way of levelling the playing field even if the law couldn't. This time, I had played my part in ensuring a group of corrupt men masquerading as police officers faced their future behind bars and I should have felt proud of myself but I didn't. I felt dirty, indelibly stained by the corruption of others. The foul acts they perpetrated would now be broadcast to the public they betrayed and serve only to fuel the prejudices of those who would never see or understand the dedication of others wearing the uniform, those of us who would never be indifferent to corruption and who would do whatever it took and bear any burden to overcome it.

46

I got a promotion to Detective Chief Inspector of the Regional Drug Squad and I knew I had a lot of things to sort out there. The squad had suffered at the hands of Cliff Ambrose and it was now up to me to put things right. I promised Molly that we'd use some of the pay increase to visit our kids overseas, but I couldn't promise when that would be. I think she understood.

Dai had got engaged again – to ex-Mrs Billy Hughes and I didn't know whether I should congratulate him or slap him for being so stupid. Something like that wouldn't have happened in my day. Back then when I met my missus, the job had total control over relationships and would never have condoned a coupling between a copper and an ex-con's ex-wife. The job had vetted prospective partners and even insisted on officers living within certain controlled areas. How times had changed. Still, Dai seemed happy enough and I sincerely hoped it would work out for them both this time.

Ron, my former DCI, retired to tend his gardens and I wondered how he'd settle into a life without the job. Anne was at last free from the shackles of the past and – the last I heard – was living life to the full. Thankfully, her sister made a good recovery too. She'd have to live with the horrors of Coulter's visit for the rest of her life, but at least she was alive and in the bosom of her loving family.

I've always thought it strange how, sometimes, the weather seemed to know what mood you were in? It was one of those days. It was pissing down and we were soaked, standing under pointless umbrellas. I stood with Dai and John Fuller at the side of an open grave and watched silently as Billy's remains were suspended above the grave with thick straps held firmly by the bearers. Billy had had a pauper's burial and was finally at rest in a simple grave in a Porthcawl cemetery. Apart from the bearers, only Dai, John and I had attended the service and we belted out the hymn as his remains were lowered to his final resting place, five years late.

* * *

We began the short walk back to the pool car we had borrowed to attend the funeral, I had a lot on my mind. There was always a lot on my mind. I never felt elated for long after solving a case. The buzz quickly wore off for me. I couldn't explain why but I suddenly felt drained and lethargic. Then I saw something moving quickly between the headstones. Dai had seen it too. "Boss, over there," shouted Dai.

I looked at where he was pointing and couldn't believe my eyes. There, leaping over the graves like a deer running from a hunter was the Dick of the Dunes. The heavy rain had no chance of soaking clothing where he was concerned.

"Fucking hell. Stop the bastard!" I shouted as I began to sprint for the first time in years.

178

The three of us raced after the naked man. I could feel my spirit soar again and a grin had formed on my face. I looked across at Dai and John. They were laughing as we chased the flasher through the graveyard like three rugby-ground stewards pursuing Erica Rowe. I knew we'd have no chance of catching him; he had too much of a lead on us. But, it finally dawned on me that this was what it was all about for me: it was the chase that I lived for and, as was the case for most police work, sometimes the chase was the best part of the hunt.

Lightning Source UK Ltd.
Milton Keynes UK
UKHW020221280519
343433UK00008B/436/P